HOUGHTON MIFFLIN

Kentucky

Experience Science

HOUGHTON MIFFLIN   BOSTON

Authors

William Badders
Director of the Cleveland
Mathematics and
Science Partnership
Cleveland Municipal
School District
Cleveland, Ohio

Douglas Carnine, Ph.D.
Professor of Education
University of Oregon
Eugene, Oregon

Bobby Jeanpierre, Ph.D.
Assistant Professor,
Science Education
University of Central Florida
Orlando, Florida

James Feliciani
Supervisor of Instructional
Media and Technology
Land O' Lakes, Florida

Carolyn Sumners, Ph.D.
Director of Astronomy
and Physical Sciences
Houston Museum
of Natural Science
Houston, Texas

Catherine Valentino
Author-in-Residence
Houghton Mifflin
West Kingston, Rhode Island

Printed in the U.S.A.

ISBN-13: 978-0-618-96602-8
ISBN 0-618-96602-1

1 2 3 4 5 6 7 8 9 VHO 14 13 12 11 10 09 08 07

Contents

The Structure of Matter

Contents

1 What Are Elements?

All matter is made up of elements. The smallest piece of an element is called an atom.

Elements and Atoms

All matter is made up of elements. An **element** is a substance that cannot be broken apart into other substances. You can think of elements as the building blocks of matter.

Some substances are made from a single element. Diamond is made from only the element carbon. Most substances are made from two or more elements.

An **atom** is the smallest particle, or piece, of an element that still has the properties, or qualities, of that element.

Atoms are so tiny they can be seen only with a special microscope. If you lined up 100 million atoms end-to-end, they might measure as long as 1 centimeter (less than an inch)!

In about 430 B.C., the Greek thinker Democritus gave the atom its name. He believed that atoms were solid and could not be changed or destroyed.

Democritus

Models of the Atom

Not all of Democritus' ideas about atoms were correct. Over time, scientists have found out things that have changed the model of the atom they use.

One scientist found that atoms have negatively charged particles called **electrons**. Another scientist showed that atoms have a small core in the middle called the **nucleus**.

The atom models on this page show how scientists' ideas about atoms have changed over the years.

Atom Models

JOHN DALTON (1803) Atoms are solid balls of different sizes and masses.

J.J. THOMSON (1897) A ball of positive charge has negatively charged electrons spaced evenly all through it.

ERNEST RUTHERFORD (1911) An atom has a small core in the middle called the nucleus. Around the nucleus is mostly empty space. Electrons move through that space.

NIELS BOHR (1913) Electrons move in exact orbits, or paths, around the nucleus

ERWIN SCHRODINGER (1926) Electron clouds, or orbitals, show how likely it is to find an electron in a certain spot. This is the most widely accepted model of the atom today.

Organization of Atoms

Electrons move quickly around the nucleus. They have a negative electrical charge and a very small mass. Most of an atom's mass is in the nucleus. The nucleus is made of protons and neutrons. A **proton** is a particle with a positive charge. A **neutron** is a particle with no charge.

Any atom of a certain element has the same number of protons in its nucleus. However, the number of neutrons may be different. A carbon atom always has six protons in its nucleus. And while most have six neutrons, some have seven or eight neutrons.

A carbon atom also has six electrons. Atoms have the same number of protons and electrons. The positive and negative charges balance each other so the atom is neutral.

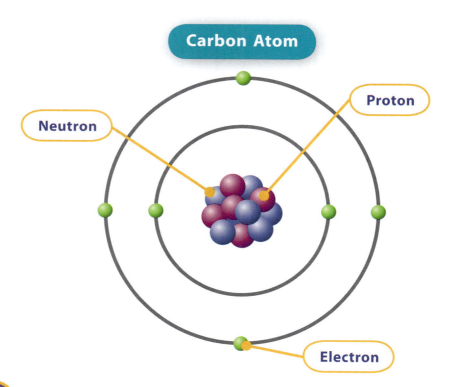

Carbon Atom

Proton

Neutron

Electron

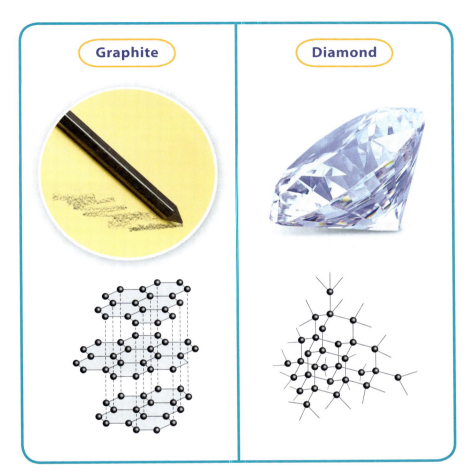

Graphite

Diamond

Carbon is found in nature in many forms with different properties. That is because carbon atoms can group together in different ways.

Graphite is a form of carbon. The "lead" in most pencils is graphite mixed with clay. In graphite, the carbon atoms are grouped in rings of six atoms each. These rings form sheets that can slide past each other. This gives graphite its slippery feel.

Diamond is another form of pure carbon. It is the hardest natural substance on Earth. That is because the carbon atoms in diamond are packed tightly together. Each atom is joined to four other atoms.

Elements Alone and Joined

As you have seen, carbon atoms can join together in different ways. Most atoms join with other atoms to form molecules. A **molecule** is two or more atoms joined together by forces called chemical bonds. In a molecule, the atoms in some ways act together as one part. Some molecules are made up of atoms of just one element. The oxygen in the air you breathe is made of molecules of two oxygen atoms.

HELIUM
The element helium in these balloons is less dense than air, so they float.

ALUMINUM
The element aluminum is a shiny metal. It is strong, but it does not weigh very much.

Other molecules are made up of atoms of more than one element. A molecule of water has two hydrogen atoms and one oxygen atom. Some molecules in your body are made of thousands, millions, or even billions of atoms!

An element's properties come from the atoms that make up that element. Some properties are color, hardness, and density. Look at the pictures of elements on these pages. What are some of the properties of the elements shown?

COPPER
The element copper is a shiny metal that can be stretched into wires.

SILVER
The element silver is a shiny metal that is soft enough to be formed into things like bracelets and rings.

COMPARE AND CONTRAST

How are atoms, molecules, and elements different?

2 What Is the Periodic Table?

Scientists have named more than 100 elements. The elements are organized, or sorted out, in the periodic table.

Organizing the Elements

Long ago, people in ancient Greece put forth the idea that all matter is made up of four elements: earth, air, fire, and water. But people began to understand that there must be more than just those four elements.

In the 1600s, an English scientist said that earth, air, fire, and water could not be real elements. In the late 1700s, a French scientist made one of the first lists of chemical elements.

By the 1800s, scientists had begun to name many new elements. They were also learning that some elements had properties that were alike. They began to organize elements into families, or groups, with properties that were alike. However, all scientists did not group elements in the same way.

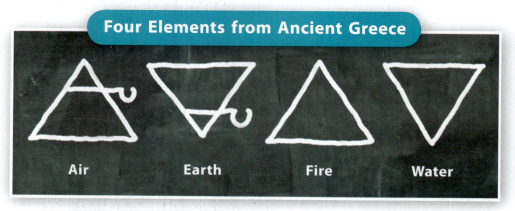

Four Elements from Ancient Greece

Air   Earth   Fire   Water

Long ago, people used these figures for what they believed were the four elements—air, earth, fire, and water.

ПЕРИОДИЧЕСКАЯ СИСТЕМА ЭЛЕМЕНТОВ

Mendeleyev grouped the elements in this table.

Mendeleyev's Table

In 1869, Russian scientist Dmitri Mendeleyev came up with a way to list and group the elements. First, he listed the elements in order of growing mass. When he studied the list, he noticed that the properties of the elements showed a repeating pattern.

Next, Mendeleyev moved elements around on the list. He put elements with properties that were alike in the same columns.

Today, scientists all over the world use a table much like Mendeleyev's table. Like his table, today's <mark>periodic table</mark> organizes elements by their properties.

Why is the table called periodic? Remember that Mendeleyev found that the properties of elements have a repeating pattern. The word *periodic* means "repeating."

Mendeleyev did not know why there was this repeating pattern. Scientists now can explain how elements in the same columns form chemical bonds in ways that are alike.

The Periodic Table

In today's periodic table, elements are listed in order of growing atomic number. The atomic number is the number of protons in an element's nucleus.

A periodic table is shown below. The box for each element lists the atomic number, chemical symbol, and name. The ==chemical symbol== is a shorter form of the element's name.

Each column in the table is called a group. Elements in a group have properties that are alike. The rows in the table are called periods. The number of elements in the periods gets larger. Notice that two rows were taken out of the table to keep the table from being too wide.

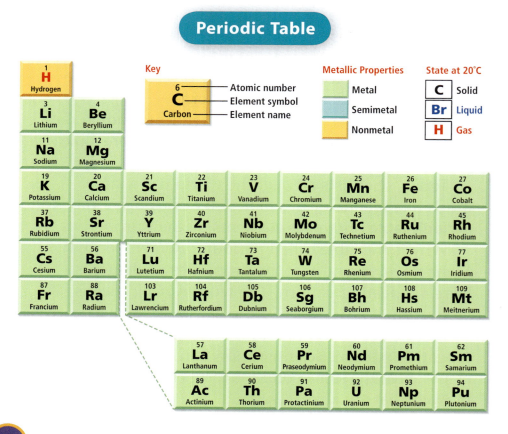

Periodic Table

Classification of Elements

Elements can be classified, or grouped, in different ways. In the table below, the colors of the boxes show whether each element is a metal, nonmetal, or semimetal.

Metals are generally shiny and can be bent or stretched. They also conduct, or move, electricity. Most elements are metals.

Many nonmetals are gases. Solid nonmetals are most often dull in color. They do not conduct electricity, bend, or stretch very much. They break easily.

Semimetals are like metals in some ways and like nonmetals in other ways.

The colors of the chemical symbols on the chart tell you if the element is a solid, liquid, or gas at room temperature. Most elements are solids.

									2 **He** Helium
			5 **B** Boron	6 **C** Carbon	7 **N** Nitrogen	8 **O** Oxygen	9 **F** Fluorine		10 **Ne** Neon
			13 **Al** Aluminum	14 **Si** Silicon	15 **P** Phosphorus	16 **S** Sulfur	17 **Cl** Chlorine		18 **Ar** Argon
28 **Ni** Nickel	29 **Cu** Copper	30 **Zn** Zinc	31 **Ga** Gallium	32 **Ge** Germanium	33 **As** Arsenic	34 **Se** Selenium	35 **Br** Bromine		36 **Kr** Krypton
46 **Pd** Palladium	47 **Ag** Silver	48 **Cd** Cadmium	49 **In** Indium	50 **Sn** Tin	51 **Sb** Antimony	52 **Te** Tellurium	53 **I** Iodine		54 **Xe** Xenon
78 **Pt** Platinum	79 **Au** Gold	80 **Hg** Mercury	81 **Tl** Thallium	82 **Pb** Lead	83 **Bi** Bismuth	84 **Po** Polonium	85 **At** Astatine		86 **Rn** Radon
110 **Ds** Darmstadtium	111 **Uuu** Unununium*								

63 **Eu** Europium	64 **Gd** Gadolinium	65 **Tb** Terbium	66 **Dy** Dysprosium	67 **Ho** Holmium	68 **Er** Erbium	69 **Tm** Thulium	70 **Yb** Ytterbium
95 **Am** Americium	96 **Cm** Curium	97 **Bk** Berkelium	98 **Cf** Californium	99 **Es** Einsteinium	100 **Fm** Fermium	101 **Md** Mendelevium	102 **No** Nobelium

* Temporary name

Metals

Look at the periodic table on pages 12 and 13. Find the red line. All the metals fall to the left of this line.

You very likely think of metals as shiny things. One of the properties that most metals have is being able to reflect, or return, light. Being able to bend is another property of most metals. People can bend a metal by using force or by heating it.

Electricity moves through copper electrical wires. Electrical wires make use of two properties of metals: Metals can be pulled into thin wires, and they can carry electricity.

You may see many things made of metals around you. Your desk might be made of steel, which is made from iron. Coins are made from copper and nickel.

Metals are also found in foods and in your body. In fact, a healthy body needs small amounts of many different metals.

Magnesium is one of the metals that makes fireworks sparkle.

This is magnesium in its element form.

Semimetals

In the periodic table, semimetals are between the metals and nonmetals. They have properties of both metals and nonmetals.

The element silicon is a semimetal. About 28 percent of Earth's crust, or outer layer, is silicon. This makes silicon Earth's second most common element. Silicon is found in most rocks, in water, and even in your body.

Like all semimetals, sometimes silicon carries electricity and other times it does not. Adding other elements to silicon can cause it to carry electricity. That is why silicon is used to make computer chips.

This is silicon in its element form.

Silicon is a semimetal that is used to make computer chips.

Phosphorus is a nonmetal that is used to make flares.

This is phosphorus in its element form.

Nonmetals and Noble Gases

Solid nonmetals are dull in color and do not carry electricity. They often break easily. Sulfur is a nonmetal. It is important in the chemical business.

Many nonmetals, such as nitrogen and oxygen, are gases. Nitrogen makes up most of the air you breathe. Oxygen makes up almost one-fourth of the air you breathe.

The last column, or group, of the periodic table is made of nonmetals only. These are the ==noble gases==, the elements that hardly ever join with other elements to form molecules.

Helium is a noble gas that is used to fill balloons because it is lighter than air. Noble gases will glow if electricity is passed through them.

CATEGORIZE

What is the difference between groups and periods in the periodic table?

3 What Are Compounds?

Two or more elements can combine, or join, to form a compound. Compounds have different properties from the elements that make them.

Combining Elements

At one time, people thought water was an element. However, an element cannot be broken down into other substances. Scientists figured out that water is not an element when they broke it down into other substances.

Water is a compound. A **compound** is a substance made up of two or more elements that are chemically joined. Water is made up of the elements hydrogen and oxygen.

A compound has its own chemical properties. In many compounds, atoms come together to form molecules. Each molecule of a compound acts in the exact same way. They all have the same chemical properties.

All water molecules are made up of two hydrogen atoms and one oxygen atom. Every molecule of water has the properties of water. These properties are different from the properties of hydrogen and oxygen.

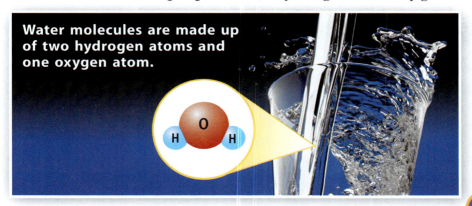

Water molecules are made up of two hydrogen atoms and one oxygen atom.

Many Compounds

Many compounds are found in nature. Scientists have made even more. There are many compounds made of two elements. Each time you breathe out, your breath has a compound called carbon dioxide. Molecules of carbon dioxide are made up of one carbon atom and two oxygen atoms.

Another compound is rust. Many things are made of steel, including cars and trucks. Steel is made mostly of the element iron. When iron is left outdoors, it will rust.

Rust is a compound called iron oxide. It is made of iron and oxygen. Iron oxide forms when iron joins with oxygen in the air. Water makes this happen even faster. That is why iron rusts more quickly when it is wet.

Other compounds are made of more than two elements. Limestone rock is mostly a compound called calcium carbonate. It is made up of calcium, carbon, and oxygen.

The rust on this truck is a compound called iron oxide.

Making and Breaking Compounds

To form a compound, the atoms of the elements in the compound must take part in a chemical reaction. A **chemical reaction** is a process in which one or more substances are changed into one or more different substances.

Sugar is a compound made up of carbon, hydrogen, and oxygen. If you heat the sugar over a flame long enough, a chemical reaction will take place. Water vapor will be let go into the air. A black substance will be left behind. This substance is carbon.

This kind of chemical reaction breaks down one substance into simpler substances. Another kind of chemical reaction joins simple substances to form a more complex substance.

Energy is an important part of all chemical reactions. Energy is needed to break apart compounds. Energy is let go when elements join to form compounds.

Chemical Reaction

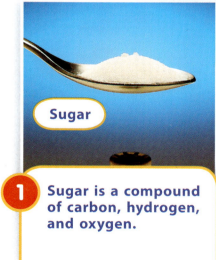

Sugar

1 Sugar is a compound of carbon, hydrogen, and oxygen.

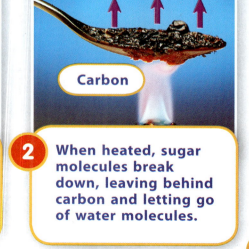

H_2O H_2O H_2O

Carbon

2 When heated, sugar molecules break down, leaving behind carbon and letting go of water molecules.

Compounds and Formulas

Scientists use chemical formulas to name chemical compounds. A **chemical formula** is a short way to describe a compound. Chemical formulas use chemical symbols to show which elements are in a compound.

The chemical symbol for iron is Fe. The chemical symbol for sulfur is S. The chemical formula for iron sulfide is FeS. This formula tells you that iron sulfide has one iron atom for every sulfur atom.

Often a compound has more of one element than another element. In such cases, the formula also has numbers placed to the lower right of the symbols. A number tells you how many atoms of that element are in the compound. The chemical formula for water is H_2O. In water, there are two hydrogen atoms for every one oxygen atom.

Making a Compound

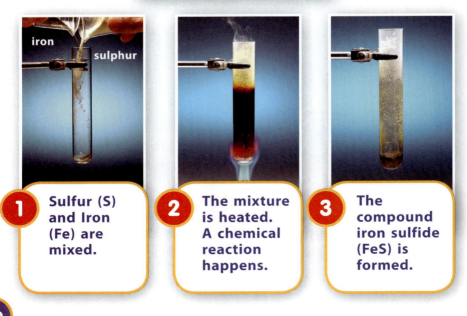

iron
sulphur

1 Sulfur (S) and Iron (Fe) are mixed.

2 The mixture is heated. A chemical reaction happens.

3 The compound iron sulfide (FeS) is formed.

Everyday Compounds

Compounds, like elements, are pure substances. Only a chemical reaction will break down a compound into its separate elements. All compounds have their own special properties.

Table salt is used to make food taste better. Salt is a compound called sodium chloride. Its chemical formula is NaCl. The properties of the compound sodium chloride, or salt, are very different from those of the elements sodium and chlorine.

As an element, sodium is a very soft, shiny metal. The element chlorine is a green colored, poisonous gas. It is used to kill germs that can hurt you. It has a strong smell. If you have ever been swimming in a pool or used bleach, you know what chlorine smells like. When sodium and chlorine meet, a chemical reaction between them makes salt, or sodium chloride.

On the next page, you will read about three more everyday compounds.

Sodium (Na) and chlorine (Cl) are the elements that make up sodium chloride (NaCl), or table salt.

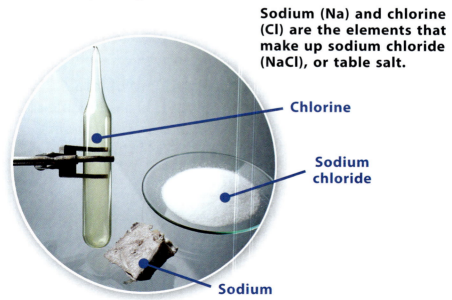

Chlorine

Sodium chloride

Sodium

Carbon Dioxide Carbon dioxide (CO_2) is a gas made up of carbon and oxygen. Every time you breathe out, your breath has carbon dioxide. Carbon dioxide is also made when almost anything that has carbon in it is burned. Some drinks get their bubbles from carbon dioxide.

Carbon dioxide gas gives soda its bubbles.

Glass Sand and glass are made mostly of a compound called silicon dioxide (SiO_2). Silicon dioxide is only one of the compounds in glass. It is mixed with other compounds and heated. The glass is shaped as it cools.

Glass is made of silicon dioxide (SiO_2) and other compounds.

Polymers Some compounds are made up of large molecules called polymers. A polymer is a molecule made up of parts that repeat. Many fats and proteins are polymers. They are important to life. Plastics are polymers, too.

The coating of this frying pan is made of a polymer.

Water: Earth's Most Common Compound

Water is everywhere on Earth. About three-fourths of Earth's surface is covered with water. All forms of life depend on water to live.

Water is different from other compounds. It is one of the few compounds that is liquid at room temperature. It is also able to dissolve, or break down, more substances than any other liquid.

One reason water has these properties is because of its shape. Water molecules have a bent shape. This gives the oxygen end of the molecule a bit of a negative charge and the hydrogen end a bit of a positive charge. These differences make water able to dissolve many compounds.

The charges also draw the hydrogen and oxygen ends of different water molecules together. This is why water is a liquid at many temperatures.

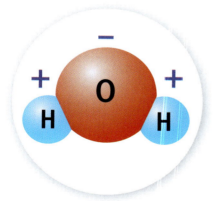

The bent shape of the water molecule gives water its special properties.

COMPARE AND CONTRAST

Name three common compounds and their uses.

Glossary

atom (AT uhm), the smallest particle of an element that still has the properties of that element

chemical formula (KEHM ih kuhl FAWR myuh luh), a shorthand way to describe the chemical makeup of a compound

chemical reaction (KEHM ih kuhl ree AK shuhn), a process in which one or more substances are changed into one or more different substances, or a specific example of one or more chemical changes

chemical symbol (KEHM ih kuhl SIHM buhl), a letter or letters that abbreviates an element's name

compound (KAHM pownd), a substance that is made up of two or more elements that are chemically combined

electron (ih LEHK trahn), a particle in an atom that has a negative charge

Glossary

element (EHL uh muhnt), a substance that cannot be broken down into other substances

metal (MEHT l), any one of the elements located on the left and bottom of the periodic table, which are usually shiny, can be bent or stretched, and conduct electricity

molecule (MAHL ih kyool), two or more atoms joined by chemical bonds

neutron (NOO trahn), a particle in the nucleus of an atom that has no charge

noble gas (NOH buhl gas), any one of the elements located in the far right column of the periodic table, which generally do not combine with other elements to form molecules

nonmetal (nahn MEHT l), elements that are usually dull, brittle, and do not conduct electricity

Glossary

nucleus (NOO klee uhs), storehouse of the cell's most important chemical information, or the central core of an atom

periodic table (pihr ee AHD ihk TAY buhl), a table that organizes the elements by their properties

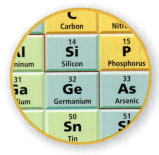

proton (PROH tahn), a particle in the nucleus of an atom that has a positive charge

semimetal (SEHM ee meht l), elements that have some properties of metals and some properties of nonmetals

Think About What You Have Read

Vocabulary

❶ Atoms of two different elements have different numbers of _____ .

A) atoms

B) compounds

C) molecules

D) protons

Comprehension

❷ Explain how diamond and graphite are alike and how they are different.

❸ What information about each element is listed in its box in the periodic table?

❹ What happens when atoms of two or more elements combine chemically?

Critical Thinking

❺ Two elements in the periodic table are liquid at room temperature. What are these elements? If they were solid at room temperature, would their placement in the periodic table be different?

Characteristics of Matter

Contents

How Can Materials Be Identified?

Physical and chemical properties are features used to describe, identify, and group matter.

Using Your Senses

Every kind of material is some form of matter. Every kind of matter has properties, or traits, that you can use to describe it. You can use your senses to help you describe some properties. You might say an ice cube is cold, has no color, and has no smell.

Properties can also be used to help identify pure substances—elements and compounds—and to tell one kind of matter from another.

Two kinds of properties can be used to describe and group matter—physical properties and chemical properties. Think about a sheet of paper and a sheet of tin foil. Both are thin, flat, and bend easily. These are physical properties. Also note that paper will burn and tin will not. Burning is a chemical property.

This basketball is round and orange. These are physical properties.

Some Properties of Materials		
Property	**Water**	**Glass**
Color	no color and clear	no color and clear
State	liquid at room temperature	solid at room temperature
Melting point	0°C (32°F)	greater than 1,000°C (1832°F)

A **physical property** can be measured or noticed by the senses. Some physical properties are state, size, color, and smell. Many physical properties, such as volume, mass, and density, can be measured.

A **chemical property** is the ability of a material to change its chemical makeup. Materials are made of much smaller parts—atoms and molecules. When there are changes in the way that the atoms and molecules are put together, a new material is formed. The new material has different properties from the first material.

You can discover a material's chemical properties by noticing how it changes when different things happen to it. When a piece of paper is held in a flame, the paper will burn. Burning is a chemical change in which matter joins with oxygen. Burning paper makes new matter that is very different from the paper and oxygen.

Mass, Volume, and Density

Mass is a measure of the amount of matter in an object or material. It can be measured in grams (g) or kilograms (kg). A large object has more matter than a smaller object made of the same material. So, the larger object has more mass.

Volume is the amount of space matter takes up. The volume of a solid can be measured in cubic centimeters (cm^3). Liquid volumes can be measured in liters (L) or milliliters (mL). One cubic centimeter is equal to one milliliter.

You can find the volume of a rectangular solid by multiplying its length, width, and height. To find the volume of a solid with an odd shape, you can put it in water in a jar with markings that measure the amount of water. The object's volume is the same as the change in the water level.

MASS The mass of an object can be measured with a balance or a scale.

VOLUME To find the volume of a solid that does not float in water, measure the change in water level.

Density is not the same as mass. The <mark>density</mark> of a material is its mass per unit volume. To find the density of a material, measure its mass and its volume. Then divide the mass by the volume. You can follow this rule to find that a 10-mL sample with a mass of 13 g has a density of 1.3 grams per milliliter (g/mL).

All amounts of an element or compound that are kept in the same way have the same density. That means that a drop of pure water and a large amount of pure water both have a density of 1 g/mL. This is the density of pure liquid water. Liquids with other densities are not pure water.

DENSITY A bottle filled with plastic foam will float. This is because foam is less dense than water. A bottle filled with sand will sink. This is because sand is denser than water.

Melting and Boiling Points

Another physical property is state of matter. The three states of matter are solid, liquid, and gas.

Solids are firm. They have an exact shape and volume. Liquids flow. They take on the shape of their container, but they keep the same volume. Gases have no real shape or volume. They can move to fill any container. They are generally much less dense than solids and liquids.

When enough energy is added to a solid, it melts to make a liquid. The temperature at which a solid changes to a liquid is called its **melting point**. When enough energy is taken away from a liquid, it freezes to make a solid. The freezing point and the melting point for a substance are the same.

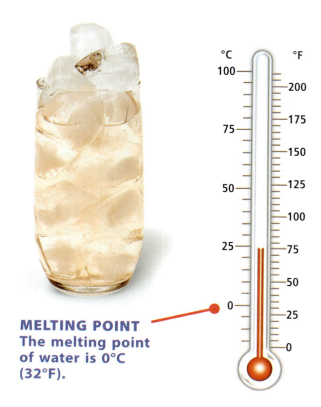

MELTING POINT
The melting point of water is 0°C (32°F).

BOILING POINT The boiling point of water is 100°C (212°F).

The melting point is the same for all samples of any given substance. So, this property can be used to identify different substances. The melting point of water is 0°C (32°F). The melting point of gold is about 1,060°C (1,940°F).

When enough energy is added to a liquid, it changes into a gas. The temperature at which this happens is called the **boiling point**.

Boiling point can also be used to identify a substance. Both water and rubbing alcohol are liquids with no color, but they have different boiling points. The boiling point of water is 100°C (212°F). The boiling point of rubbing alcohol is 108°C (226°F).

Solubility

If you stir sugar in water, you can see the sugar dissolve in the water, or mix evenly with it. This mixture is called a solution. You will learn more about solutions later in this book.

The measure of how much of one substance can dissolve in another is called **solubility**. Solubility is another physical property of matter. Some substances, such as salt and sugar, are very soluble in water. Other substances, such as oil and sand, are not. And while salt is soluble in water, it is not soluble in alcohol. You could use this property to tell the difference between samples of salt and sugar.

Solubility

Oil and sand will not dissolve in water.

Powdered drink mix will dissolve in water. The two make a colored solution when mixed.

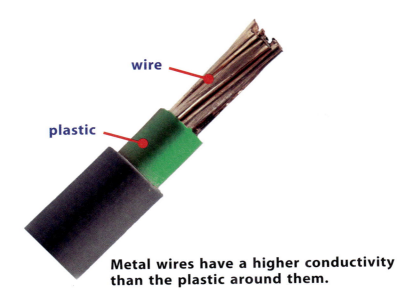

wire

plastic

Metal wires have a higher conductivity than the plastic around them.

Conductivity

Another physical property of matter is conductivity. The <mark>conductivity</mark> of a material is its ability to carry energy. Electrical conductivity has to do with carrying electricity. Thermal conductivity has to do with carrying heat.

Most metals are good conductors of both electricity and heat. Copper is used both in pots and pans and in electrical wires.

Materials that have low conductivity, such as rubber and plastic, are used to protect conductors. In an electric cord, plastic around the metal wire keeps the electricity and heat from leaving.

MAIN IDEA AND DETAILS

Compare the properties of two examples of matter.

How Does Matter Change?

A chemical change has to do with a change in the kind of matter. A physical change does not change the kind of matter.

Physical Changes

If you have sawed wood, you have seen a physical change in matter. The sawdust on the floor looks different from the wood. But the chemical makeup of the wood has not changed at all.

A **physical change** is a change in the size, shape, or state of matter. No new material is formed. In the case of the sawed wood, only the size of the matter has been changed. The chemical properties of the sawdust are the same as the chemical properties of the wood from which it came.

Cutting wood is a physical change.

Burning wood is an example of a chemical change.

Chemical Changes

A **chemical change** is a change in matter that brings about new substances. In all kinds of matter, forces called chemical bonds hold atoms or molecules together. In chemical changes, these bonds are broken and new bonds form. This brings about new substances with new chemical properties.

A **chemical reaction** is a specific example of one or more chemical changes. All chemical changes happen because of chemical reactions. Burning wood is a chemical change. A part of wood is made up of carbon, hydrogen, and oxygen. When wood burns, the atoms of carbon and hydrogen in the wood join with molecules of oxygen in the air. A chemical change forms carbon dioxide gas, water, and ashes.

Chemical changes take place all around you every day. A change in color is sometimes a sign of a chemical change. Some chemical changes give off energy in the form of heat or light.

Classifying Changes

When matter changes in the way it looks, has it gone through a chemical change? Not always. A block of ice looks very different from a puddle of water. But a change of state is a physical change.

Each molecule of ice is made up of atoms. When ice melts, the atoms in the molecules do not change. Instead, they break apart from one another and move more freely.

When water evaporates, the molecules speed up and move farther apart. The way that the molecules move has changed, but the molecules have not changed.

Dissolving is another physical change. When salt dissolves in water, salt molecules move apart and spread through the water. The molecules that make up the salt and water do not change. Other examples of physical changes are cutting and tearing.

Physical Changes

Salt dissolves in water.

The salt seems to disappear.

When water evaporates, the salt remains. Evaporation and dissolving are physical changes.

batter

muffin

CHEMICAL CHANGE When you bake muffin batter,
a chemical change happens.

Remember that a chemical change forms new substances with new chemical properties. Such changes can take place slowly or quickly, loudly or quietly, or at very hot or cold temperatures.

Rusting of iron is a slow chemical change. It happens when iron is left out in wet air. The iron joins with oxygen from the air to form iron oxide, or rust. Rust is different from either iron or oxygen.

Other chemical reactions take place quickly. When you heat muffin batter, it goes through chemical reactions that change it into muffins. The substances and their properties are different before and after the baking.

The speed at which chemical reactions take place can be changed. Adding salt to iron speeds up rusting. Raising the temperature is another way to speed up many chemical reactions.

Conservation of Matter

Whether there is a chemical or physical change, the amount of matter stays the same. When matter changes, mass is always conserved. That means that matter is neither made nor destroyed.

In a chemical change, this means that the mass of the materials before a chemical change is equal to the mass after the change. This is true even if you cannot see the materials that form, such as when a gas is made.

Matter is also conserved in all physical changes. When you place water in the freezer, there is a physical change. The water freezes and becomes ice.

As you may know, the volume of water gets bigger when it freezes. But that does not mean that matter was made. Instead, the water molecules have moved around, and they take up more space in ice than in water.

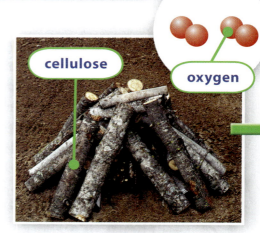

Chemical Change

cellulose

oxygen

FIRST MATERIALS
Wood is mostly made of cellulose. When it is heated, it reacts with oxygen in the air.

Sometimes the conservation of mass is hard to see. When a log burns, only a few ashes are left behind. The pictures on these two pages show and describe what happens when wood burns.

What if you could measure the mass of the logs and the oxygen? You would find that the amount of their masses added together is the same as the total mass of the ashes and gases that form when the log is burned.

water vapor

carbon dioxide

CHEMICAL CHANGE
Cellulose and oxygen join to form two gases: carbon dioxide and water vapor. The flames are hot, glowing gases.

NEW MATERIALS
Most of the wood has been changed into gases. Some carbon remains in the ashes.

CLASSIFY

How is a chemical change different from a physical change?

3 What Are Solutions and Mixtures?

Some mixtures are evenly mixed. Other mixtures have different amounts of materials in different places. Mixtures whose molecules are evenly mixed are called solutions.

Types of Mixtures

Look at the salad on this page. Each vegetable adds to its good taste. Yet if you ate different parts of the salad, you would taste each vegetable by itself. That is because a salad is a mixture. A **mixture** is a physical combination of two or more substances. The substances in a mixture are not chemically joined as they are in a compound.

Mixtures are either heterogeneous or homogeneous. In a heterogeneous mixture, such as a salad, materials are not spread out evenly. Separate pieces are present in some parts and not in others. A homogeneous mixture is the same all the way through. A sample taken from one part is exactly the same as a sample taken from any other part.

A salad is a
heterogeneous mixture.

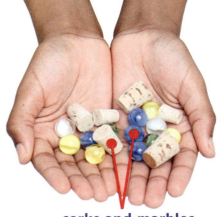

corks and marbles

The physical properties of the different parts of a mixture can help you to separate a mixture.

Separating a Mixture

In a mixture, each part keeps its own properties. If you separated all the parts of a salad, the tomatoes would still be tomatoes, and so on.

Mixtures can be separated according to different properties. Think about a mixture of corks and marbles. You could spend a lot of time picking out the corks. However, because cork floats in water, you can separate the mixture by putting it in water and removing the corks.

Mixture or Compound?

Mixtures that are alike can be made of the same materials, but in different amounts. Two salads can both have lettuce and carrots, but one may have more carrots. Two of the same compounds, however, always have the same materials in the same amounts. Every molecule of water has one oxygen atom and two hydrogen atoms. This is described in its chemical formula.

Solutions

A **solution** is a homogeneous mixture. That means it has two or more substances that are spread evenly all through the mixture. The materials that make up a solution mix together at the level of their atoms or molecules.

You make a solution when you make lemonade from a powdered mix. Some particles that mix in the water are molecules of sugar and coloring.

In any solution, the substance being dissolved is called the **solute**. The substance that dissolves the solute is called the **solvent**. In a solution of water and sugar, water is the solvent and sugar is the solute. In a solution, the properties of the substances that make up the mixture do not change when they are mixed together.

When iodine crystals are added to alcohol, they begin to dissolve.

In a short time, the solution is purple.

alcohol

iodine

Many solutions have a liquid solvent and solid solute. However, solutions can have other kinds of solvents and solutes. Soda water is a solution made of carbon dioxide gas dissolved in water. Air is a solution of different gases. Brass is a solution of two solids— zinc and copper.

Particles in a solution spread evenly through the solution because they mix at the level of their atoms or molecules. Look at the pictures on this page. When iodine and alcohol are mixed, the iodine dissolves in the alcohol. The particles of iodine spread all through the mixture. The molecules of the two substances have become evenly mixed.

Separating a Solution

To separate a solution, you must use the properties of the mixed materials. You generally cannot use the size of the particles, because they are so small. It is hard to trap and separate them.

There are other properties you can use, however. Some liquids evaporate at low temperatures. You often can allow a liquid solvent to evaporate, leaving the solute behind.

This happens when a sample of saltwater is left in the air over a couple of days. The water slowly evaporates, leaving behind solid salt.

Salt is taken from seawater through evaporation, which separates the parts of the solution.

First, the sugar cane plant is cut.

Then the sugar cane is crushed.

A simple way to separate most solutions is to use the different boiling points or melting points of the substances. Sugar is gathered in this way. Sugar cane is a plant. People who grow sugar cane cut down the sugar cane stems and crush them. Then the sugar cane juice is gathered and heated. The water boils off at 100°C (212°F), while solid sugar remains behind.

Sugar cane juice is a solution of sugar and water.

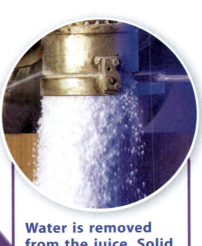

Water is removed from the juice. Solid sugar is left behind.

Alloys

Mixtures of two or more metals are called alloys. Alloys may also be mixtures of a metal and another solid. Alloys often have some of the properties of each of the materials that form them.

Bronze is an alloy of copper and tin. It has the best properties of both metals. Bronze is a strong alloy. It is also easy to hammer into thin sheets that can be formed into different shapes.

The amounts of each material in an alloy can change its properties. Steel is an alloy of iron, carbon, and sometimes other solids. Softer steels are made with less carbon. Harder steels are made with more carbon.

Brass is an alloy of copper and zinc. It is used to make many musical instruments.

COMPARE AND CONTRAST

Compare mixtures and compounds.

Glossary

boiling point (BOY lihng point), temperature at which a substance changes from a liquid to a gas

chemical change (KEHM ih kuhl chaynj), change in matter that results in new substances being formed

chemical property (KEHM ih kuhl PRAHP uhr tee), ability of a material to change its chemical makeup

chemical reaction (KEHM ih kuhl ree AK shuhn), a process in which one or more substances are changed into one or more different substances, or a specific example of one or more chemical changes

conductivity (kuhn duhk TIHV ih tee), ability to carry energy

density (DEHN sih tee), mass per unit volume of a substance

melting point (MEHL tihng point), temperature at which a substance changes from a solid to a liquid

Glossary

mixture (MIHKS chur), physical combination of two or more substances

physical change (FIHZ ih kuhl chaynj), change in the size, shape, or state of matter with no new matter being formed

physical property (FIHZ ih kuhl PRAHP uhr tee), characteristic that can be measured or detected by the senses

solubility (sahl yuh BIHL ih tee), measure of how much of one substance can dissolve in another substance

solute (SAHL yoot), substance that is dissolved in a solution

solution (suh LOO shuhn), mixture of two or more substances that are evenly distributed throughout the mixture

solvent (SAHL vuhnt), substance that dissolves the solute in a solution

Think About What You Have Read

Vocabulary

❶ The _____ of a material is the temperature at which it changes from a solid to a liquid.

A) solubility

B) melting point

C) boiling point

D) critical temperature

Comprehension

❷ How are physical and chemical properties of matter useful?

❸ What happens to substances during a chemical change?

❹ How are solutions different from other mixtures?

Critical Thinking

❺ A mixture of iodine and alcohol sits in an open beaker. Over time, purple iodine crystals form on the beaker's sides. Did they form from physical or chemical changes? Explain.

Changes of State

Contents

What Are Three States of Matter?

Matter comes in three states: solids, liquids, and gases. These states are the result of the motion and arrangement of particles.

Solids, Liquids, and Gases

Picture a huge iceberg floating in the ocean water. What you see are two states of matter. A **state of matter** is the physical form that matter takes. Three well-known states of matter are solids, liquids, and gases.

Ice is a solid state of matter. Ice is the solid form of water. Water is the liquid state of water. The air above the water is a mixture of gases that you cannot see. One of these gases is water vapor. Water vapor is the gas state of water.

STATES OF MATTER
Water can be in a solid, liquid, or gas state. In each state, the particles, or small pieces, of matter are arranged in a certain way.

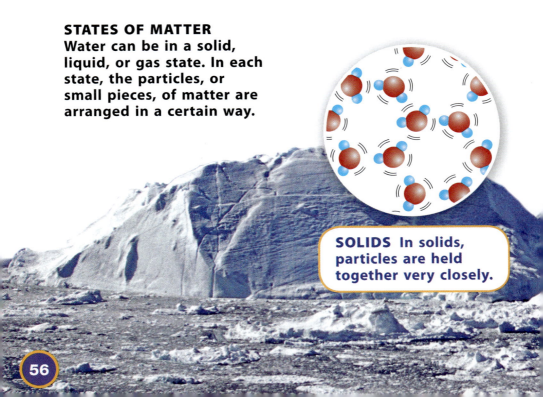

SOLIDS In solids, particles are held together very closely.

Particles and States of Matter

All matter is made up of atoms and molecules. These particles are always moving.

The state of matter depends on the movement and spacing of its particles. For most solids, particles are held closely together. They move back and forth a little, but they do not move around one another.

In liquids, particles are close together, but they have some space in which to move. They can slip past one another. That means the arrangement of particles in liquids is always changing.

In gases, particles are spread far apart. Their arrangements have no order. They fill the space of their containers. They are always bouncing off one another and the sides of their containers.

Some kinds of matter can be found in any of the three states. Others are found in only one state.

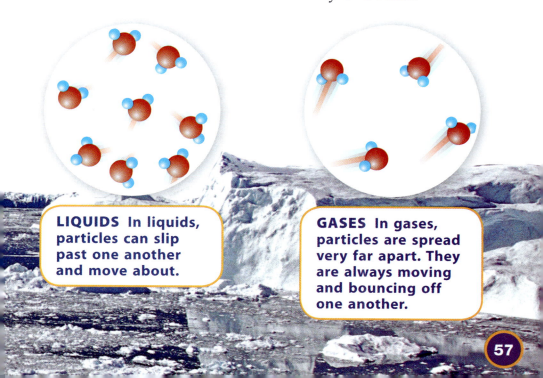

LIQUIDS In liquids, particles can slip past one another and move about.

GASES In gases, particles are spread very far apart. They are always moving and bouncing off one another.

Solids

A **solid** is a form of matter that has a definite shape and volume. The way that particles in solids are arranged and the way they move back and forth in place give solids their properties. One property is that solids keep their shapes. If you move a solid or place it into a container, its shape will stay the same.

Wood is a solid. A block of wood will keep its shape wherever you put it.

Particles in a solid are very close together. There are also small forces of attraction between them. These two things keep the particles from moving around. Because the particles stay in place, the shape of a solid does not change. This property of solids is usually called having a definite shape.

This hockey player is wearing matter in its solid form for protection. Solids always keep their shape.

You can squeeze a foam ball because of the air inside it. The solid parts of the foam keep the same size and shape.

Another property of solids is that they have definite volume. That is, they take up the same amount of space wherever they are placed. The volume of a solid object stays the same unless you remove a part of the object.

Think about a wood block. It has a certain volume. Wherever you move the block, the volume will stay the same. You can even squeeze the block, and its volume will not change much, if at all.

Many solids might seem to change shape and volume. For example, you can squeeze a foam ball into a smaller volume. A pillow changes shape when you rest your head on it. In both cases, however, solid matter is surrounded by "pockets" of air. The air changes its shape and volume. The solid parts do not.

Liquids

What shape is orange juice? You cannot say, because orange juice is a liquid. A liquid is a form of matter that has a definite volume but no definite shape. A **liquid** will change its shape to match the shape of its container.

Think about what happens when you use a straw to drink orange juice from a container. The juice has one shape in the container and a different shape when it's in the straw.

Liquids have no definite shape because their particles are not held in place. The particles of a liquid are able to flow past one another. This allows a liquid to take on the shape of its container.

Volume

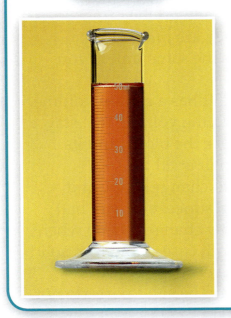

Like solids, each liquid has a volume that does not change. Think about pouring a liquid into bottles of different shapes. Each time, the liquid takes on the shape of the bottle, but the liquid's volume never changes.

Also like solids, liquids are not easy to compress, or squeeze. Because the molecules are close together, liquids do not squeeze into smaller volumes very easily.

This property makes liquids very useful. For example, some tools use a liquid to carry a force. If you push on one end of the liquid in a sealed tube, the liquid carries the push to the other end of the tube. The brakes on a car use this property. Liquid carries the force from the driver's foot on the brake to the brake pad on the wheel of the car.

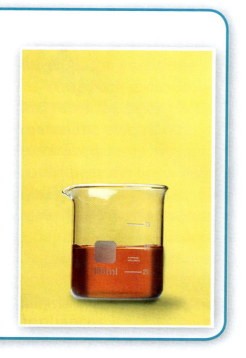

The same liquid poured into different containers will take the shape of each container. But its volume will stay the same.

Gases

A <mark>gas</mark> is a form of matter that has no definite shape or volume. The particles in gases can move about freely. Particles of a gas are always moving and bouncing off one another.

When a gas is placed in a closed container, the particles spread out to fill the container. They take the shape of the container.

Gases are easy to compress. Their particles are very far apart, so they can be pressed close together into a smaller volume.

Compressibility

Gases can be compressed into smaller and smaller volumes. Their particles are far apart, so they can be squeezed together.

Less Compressed

Somewhat Compressed

Very Compressed

To understand how gases are compressed and take the shape of containers, think about helium gas. Helium gas is often compressed inside a metal tank. It takes the shape and volume of the tank. If you use the helium to fill balloons, the gas takes on the different shapes and volumes of the balloons.

Gases have much lower densities than liquids and solids. A balloon filled with helium will float in air. This is because the helium gas in the balloon is less dense than the gases in the air.

Objects with lower densities float in liquids that have higher densities. For example, solid ice has a lower density than liquid water. That is why an ice cube floats in a glass of water.

TEXT STRUCTURE

How do a solid, a liquid, and a gas fill a container?

States of Matter

Property	Solid	Liquid	Gas
Definite Shape	yes	no	no
Definite Volume	yes	yes	no
Compressible	no	no	yes
Particle Spacing	close	close	varies

The state of matter depends on the spacing and movement of particles.

2 How Does Matter Change State?

Matter can change from one state to another state. This happens when energy is added or removed. Changes of state are always physical changes.

Melting and Freezing

Think about what happens to an ice cube when you take it out of a freezer on a hot day. The temperature is warm outside the freezer. The ice begins changing state from solid to liquid. A change of state is a physical change. In a physical change, a substance stays the same substance. It does not lose any matter.

When energy is added to a solid, its temperature rises to a certain point. The solid starts **melting**, or changing from a solid to a liquid. This happens at the substance's melting point.

The process is reversed when energy is taken from a liquid. The temperature drops to the freezing point. The temperature stays the same while the liquid freezes.

For any substance, the melting point and the freezing point are the same.

A change of state takes place when snow and ice melt. They change from solids to liquids.

Vaporizing and Condensing

Adding energy to a substance makes its particles speed up. This raises the temperature. At a certain point, the particles have so much energy that they cannot stay in the liquid state. The liquid vaporizes. **Vaporization** is the change of state from a liquid to a gas.

Rapid vaporization is called boiling. The boiling point of a substance is the temperature at which it boils.

Slow vaporization is called **evaporation**. It takes place at the surface of a liquid. A higher temperature around the liquid makes evaporation happen faster.

When energy is taken from a gas, condensation occurs. **Condensation** is a change of state from a gas to a liquid. You can see condensation on the water bottle in the picture. Water vapor in the air condensed into tiny drops on the bottle.

The water droplets on this bottle came from the condensation of water vapor in the air.

Skipping a Step

Different kinds of matter change states at different temperatures. They also change states at different rates.

Sometimes matter skips the liquid state! When conditions are right, adding energy to a solid changes it to a gas. The process of changing from a solid to a gas is called **sublimation**.

Sublimation explains why dry ice is "dry." Dry ice is made from solid carbon dioxide. The carbon dioxide does not melt into a liquid. Instead it changes into a gas. Regular ice can make things wet. Dry ice keeps things cold but does not make them wet.

The opposite of sublimation is deposition. **Deposition** is the change of state from a gas to a solid. Frost is an example of deposition. Frost is made of tiny ice crystals. It forms on freezing-cold surfaces. When water vapor in the air touches these surfaces, the vapor changes from a gas to a solid.

DEPOSITION When energy is taken from water vapor in the air, frost can form on a freezing-cold window.

SUBLIMATION Sometimes a solid changes to a gas without going through the liquid state. Solid carbon dioxide changes into a gas.

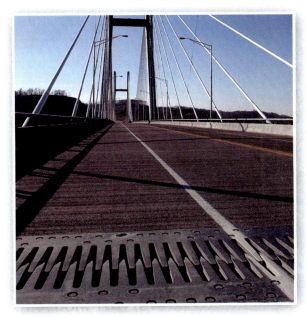

EXPANSION JOINTS in bridges reduce the effects of expansion and contraction. These joints make bridges safer.

Expansion and Contraction

Most solid matter will expand, or increase in size, when it is heated. This increase in size due to heat is called ==thermal expansion==.

Recall that the particles of solids can move back and forth a little. When a solid gets warm, its particles move more quickly. They also move farther apart. As a result, the matter in the solid expands.

When most solids are cooled, the opposite happens. The particles move even more slowly. The matter contracts, or decreases in size. This is called thermal contraction. Thermal contraction makes a solid take up less space.

Thermal expansion and contraction can make bridges dangerous. The solids expand and contract. Bridges may become weak or even break. Builders add spaces in bridges called expansion joints. These joints allow bridges to change length safely.

Not all substances get smaller when they get colder. Water expands when it freezes. The particles in ice are spread farther apart than the particles in liquid water.

Expansion of water explains why ice floats. A given mass of ice has a greater volume than an equal mass of liquid water. This means that the solid ice is less dense than the liquid water.

Heating or cooling can change the volume of matter. The mass will always stay the same. One gram of a solid, a liquid, or a gas remains one gram at any temperature.

CAUSE AND EFFECT

How does temperature affect the motion of particles that make up a substance?

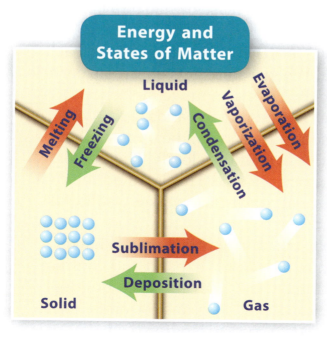

Energy and States of Matter

Liquid

Melting

Freezing

Evaporation

Vaporization

Condensation

Sublimation

Deposition

Solid

Gas

Changes in energy can cause changes in state.

Glossary

condensation (kahn dehn SAY shuhn), change of state from a gas to a liquid as energy is removed

deposition (dehp uh ZIHSH uhn), change of state from a gas to a solid

evaporation (ih VAP uh ray shuhn), the change in state from a liquid to a gas; slow or gradual vaporization

gas (gas), state of matter that has no definite shape or volume

liquid (LIHK wihd), state of matter that has a definite volume, but no definite shape

melting (MEHL tihng), change of state from a solid to a liquid as energy is added

Glossary

solid (SAHL ihd), state of matter that has a definite shape and volume

state of matter (stayt uhv MAT uhr), physical form that matter takes; gas, liquid, and solid

sublimation (suhb luh MAY shuhn), change of state from a solid to a gas

thermal expansion (THUHR muhl ihk SPAN shuhn), increase in size of a substance due to a change in temperature

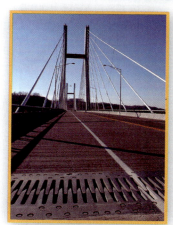

vaporization (vay puh rih ZAY shuhn), change of state from a liquid to a gas as energy is added

Think About What You Have Read

Vocabulary

❶ Solid, liquid, and gas are three _____ .

A) properties of matter

B) states of matter

C) particles of matter

D) laws of matter

Comprehension

❷ Name three changes of state that can take place when energy is taken from a substance.

❸ What two factors determine the state of matter of an object or sample?

❹ Compare the arrangement of particles in a solid, a liquid, and a gas.

Critical Thinking

❺ Describe three different kinds of matter that could be used to fill a mattress. Use one example of each state. Which would you prefer for your mattress? Explain.

Forces, Motion, and Work

Contents

1

What Can Change an Object's Motion?

A force applied to an object can change the object's motion.

Motion

When something moves, it is in motion. **Motion** is a change in an object's position. A motionless object is at rest, or stationary.

How do you know if an object is moving or is at rest? You observe that object in relation to another object. This is called a frame of reference.

Imagine people on a sidewalk. They watch a bus drive past. Their frame of reference includes other objects, such as trees and houses. These people are stationary in relation to these objects. The bus moves in relation to these objects.

Riders on the bus have their own frame of reference. It's the bus and everything inside it. Riders are not moving in relation to the bus, unless they get up and move.

ON THE BUS
Bus riders are stationary in their frame of reference.

ON THE GROUND People standing on the sidewalk see a bus moving from their frame of reference.

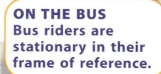

Newton's First Law

Sir Isaac Newton discovered much of what we know about motion. Newton described several laws of motion in 1687. His laws show how forces and motion are connected. A **force** is a push or a pull that acts on an object.

Newton's first law of motion states that an object at rest remains at rest. An outside force must act on it to make it move. Likewise, an object in motion stays in motion. It moves at a constant speed in the same direction if no forces act on it. This resistance to a change in motion is called **inertia**.

A soccer game shows how inertia works. The soccer ball sits at rest on the field. It has inertia. A player kicks it. It rolls or flies in the air. Outside forces then start to slow it down or make it fall.

The player kicks the ball and sets it in motion.

Speed, Velocity, and Acceleration

Newton's first law explains that an outside force is needed to change an object's speed or direction. **Speed** is a measure of distance moved in a given amount of time.

To calculate average speed, divide the distance traveled by the time it took the object to travel that distance. You can use a formula to relate speed (s), distance (d), and time (t):

$$s = d/t$$

For example, if a car travels 160 km (100 mi) in 2 hours, its average speed is

$$s = 160 \; km/2 \; h$$
$$s = 80 \; km/h$$

There are many other units of speed. However, they all are written as units of distance per units of time. Meters per second (m/s) is one common unit.

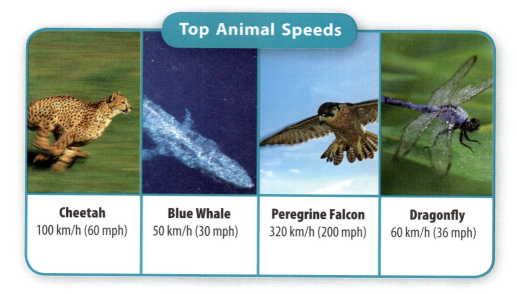

Top Animal Speeds

Cheetah	Blue Whale	Peregrine Falcon	Dragonfly
100 km/h (60 mph)	50 km/h (30 mph)	320 km/h (200 mph)	60 km/h (36 mph)

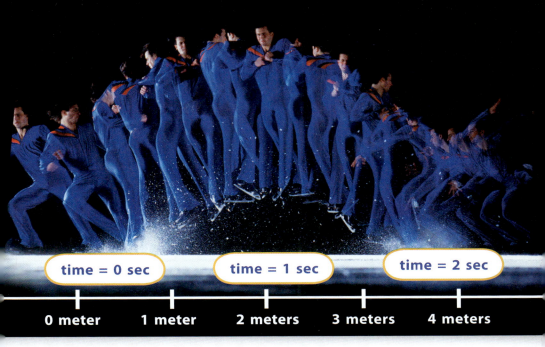

0 meter 1 meter 2 meters 3 meters 4 meters

This stop-action photo shows how a skating jump causes changes in acceleration and velocity. If a skater moves a distance of 4 meters during 2 seconds, what is his average speed?

Velocity is a measure of both an object's speed *and* its direction. How are speed and velocity different?

Imagine you and a friend both go jogging. You both run at a speed of 8 km/h (5 mph). But you run north, and she runs south. Your speed is the same, but not your velocity. You are going different directions.

Whenever an object's speed or direction changes, its velocity changes, too. This change is called **acceleration**. Acceleration measures a change in speed, in direction, or both over a certain period of time.

For example, suppose a car's velocity changes from 13 m/s to 23 m/s in 5 seconds. The change in the car's velocity is 23 m/s − 13 m/s = 10 m/s. It takes 5 s to make this change. So, the acceleration is 10 m/s ÷ 5 s = 2 m/s per second.

Balanced and Unbalanced Forces

Imagine playing tug-of-war with a dog. You pull on one end of the rope. The dog pulls on the other end in the opposite direction. If each of you pulls with equal force, the rope will not move. The two forces are equal in strength, but opposite in direction. The forces are balanced. Balanced forces cancel, or cross out, each other.

A friend comes to help you pull. Together, you pull with a greater force than the dog does. The forces are unbalanced. The difference between the two forces is called the net force. The net force acts on the rope. It moves in the direction of the net force—toward you.

UNBALANCED FORCES A second child adds more tugging force. Now the forces are unbalanced. The rope accelerates, or changes motion. The children pull it toward them.

BALANCED FORCES The child and the dog apply equal force in the tug-of-war. Their forces are balanced. The rope does not accelerate, or change motion.

Newton's Second Law

An object accelerates, or changes its motion, only when an unbalanced force acts on it. This is Newton's second law of motion. The law can be stated as a formula:

$$F = ma$$

F is the applied net force, m is the mass of the object, and a is the amount of acceleration. If you know two parts of the formula, you can use it to calculate the third part.

Force is measured in a unit called the newton. One **newton (N)** is the force required to accelerate a mass of 1 kg at 1 m/s per second.

Look at the photos. How does the wagon's movement change as the rider's mass changes? How does it change as the pusher's mass changes? Acceleration increases as the applied net force (push on the wagon) increases. Likewise, objects (riders) with greater mass have smaller acceleration than objects with smaller mass.

Newton's Second Law

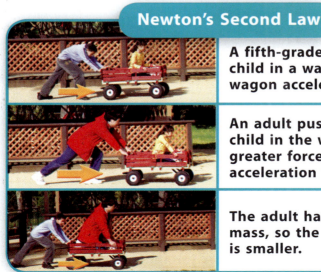

A fifth-grader pushes a child in a wagon. The wagon accelerates.

An adult pushes the child in the wagon with greater force. The wagon's acceleration is greater.

The adult has more mass, so the acceleration is smaller.

Gravity and Friction

==Gravity== is a force that causes objects with mass to be attracted, or pulled, toward one another. Gravity is a noncontact force. This means it acts on an object without touching it.

Newton also came up with a law to explain gravity. It is called the Law of Universal Gravitation. Gravity increases with the masses of the two objects. However, as the objects get farther apart, gravity pulls with weaker force. Earth's mass is much greater than the mass of any object on its surface. That's why gravity pulls you toward Earth.

The force of gravity will pull this runner back to the track.

The force of gravity accelerates the skater as she rolls downhill.

To slow down, the skater brakes. The brakes increase friction between the sidewalk and the skates.

==Friction== is a force that resists motion of one surface across another surface. Friction is a contact force. It happens when objects or surfaces touch one another. Friction is usually greater between rough surfaces than smooth ones.

In the photo, the slowing force of friction happens between the ground and the skate wheels. If the skater uses her breaks, friction increases. She will stop sooner. Air resistance, or drag, will also help slow down the skater. This kind of friction resists motion through air.

MAIN IDEA

Explain some forces that affect motion on Earth.

2

How Are Simple Machines Used?

Simple machines allow you to do the same work more easily.

Doing Work

You might think of "work" as washing dishes or walking the dog. In the last lesson, you learned about force. In science, work is related to force. **Work** is done when a force moves an object over a distance.

At times, you apply a force to something, but it does not move. Why not? Another equal force must be opposing, or pushing back against, your force. Newton's laws of motion state this.

In the first photo below, one person pushes a car. He applies force, but the car does not move. No work is done. In the second photo, two people push. Together, they apply enough force to move the car. They do work.

This person applies too little force to move the car. He is unable to do work by himself.

Two people apply the force needed to move the car over a distance. Together, they do work.

You can use a formula to calculate work done:
$$W = Fd$$
Work (W) equals the amount of force (F) times the distance (d) that the object is moved.

The standard unit for work is a newton-meter (N·m). If you apply a force of 10 N to lift a book a distance of 1 m, you have done 10 N·m of work. Another name for a newton-meter is the joule (J).

Simple Machines

Machines are tools that make work easier. A **simple machine** has few or no moving parts. It makes work easier by changing the amount of force applied, the direction of the force, or both. The six types of simple machines are shown below.

A machine does work when you apply a force. This is called an effort force. The force it overcomes is called the load, or resistance force.

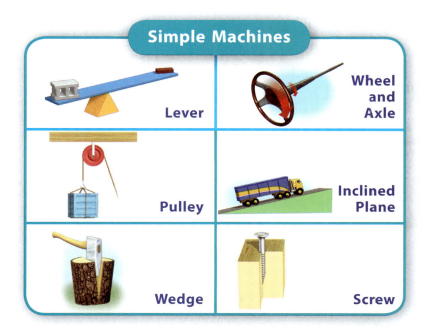

Simple Machines

Lever

Wheel and Axle

Pulley

Inclined Plane

Wedge

Screw

The load force works against the effort force.

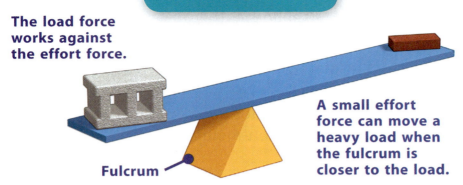

Fulcrum

A small effort force can move a heavy load when the fulcrum is closer to the load.

Levers

Levers are rigid bars that pivot, or turn, around a point. Levers can change the direction of a force. When you push down on a lever, it lifts a load. Levers can also change the ratio between force and distance an object moves. Or they can do both.

How do levers work? Look at the drawing. Effort force (the small brick) pushes down one end of the lever. A load (the large block) is lifted at the other end. The bar's pivot point is called the fulcrum.

The fulcrum sits between the effort and the load. The effort end pushes a long distance. The load rises a short distance. When the fulcrum is closer to the load, less force is needed to lift the load.

A pliers is made of two levers joined at the fulcrum. The placement of the fulcrum causes the force on the nut to be much greater than the force you use on the handles.

Pliers

Wheel and Axles and Pulleys

The wheel and axle is a simple machine that changes the amount of force applied to an object. A steering wheel, a doorknob, and a faucet are all examples of wheels and axles.

If you apply effort force to the wheel, force increases. If you apply effort force to the axle, distance over which the force acts is increased. Look at the picture of the steering wheel. Turning the wheel and axle provides force needed to turn the car wheels.

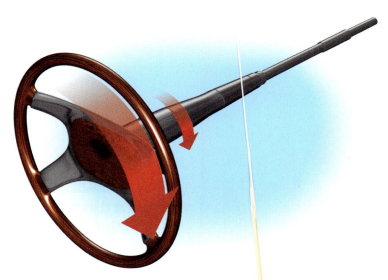

The steering wheel on a car is a wheel and axle. The axle is a cylinder connected to the center of the wheel.

A pulley is a wheel with an edge that a rope fits into. A single fixed pulley stays in place where it connects to a high point. You tie one end of the rope to the load, pass the rope over the wheel, and pull down on the other end.

The fixed pulley changes the direction of the force, but not the size of the force. If you pull the rope a distance of 1 m, the load is lifted 1 m. The force is the same. However, the pulley lets you pull down to lift a load, which is easier.

Another kind of pulley is the movable pulley. A movable pulley does reduce the force needed to lift a load. The pulley connects to the load. This doubles the pulling force. But you must pull twice as much rope to lift the load.

You can use two or more pulleys together to make a pulley system. Look at the picture of a pulley system. The more pulleys in the system, the less force you need to lift a load. However, you will need to pull more rope to lift the load.

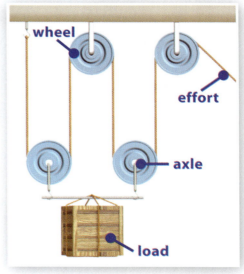

SINGLE FIXED PULLEY
A fixed pulley changes the direction, but not the amount, of the force needed to move an object.

PULLEY SYSTEM **In this system of four pulleys, pulling through 4 meters of rope will lift the load 1 meter high.**

box is lifted 2 m

box is moved 4 m

INCLINED PLANE Force applied by two people is required to lift the object straight into the truck. Using the ramp, one person applies enough force to move the object to the same height.

Inclined Planes

An inclined plane, or ramp, allows you to lift a load using less force. However, it increases the distance that you must move the object to reach a given height. The longer the ramp, the less force is required for lifting.

The pictures show two ways to lift a box into a truck. The person who uses a ramp moves the box twice the distance as the men who lift it. But he uses only half the effort force. Both methods involve the same amount of work. The men lift the box 2 m. They must apply a force equal to the weight of the box, or 500 N. So, W = 500 N × 2.0 m = 1,000 N·m.

The man on the ramp uses half the force, or 250 N. The ramp is 4.0 m long. So, W = 250 N × 4.0 m = 1,000 N·m. The example ignores friction. Friction would have an effect in the real world.

Wedges and Screws

A wedge is a simple machine that uses two inclined planes placed back to back. It changes the direction of effort force. You apply force to the thick end of the wedge to push it under or through an object. The force

changes to a sideways force as the wedge goes through the object. This sideways force is greater than the applied force. Many tools are wedges, including chisels and knives.

WEDGE An ax works as a wedge to split wood into pieces.

A screw is an inclined plane wrapped around a cylinder or cone. The plane makes up the threads of a screw. A screw changes both the direction of force and the ratio of force to distance. The screw moves forward as it is turned many times. Threads on the screw make it turn. Look at the picture of the car jack to see how a screw works.

SCREW Turning the screw pulls the diagonal parts of a car jack closer together. This raises the jack and lifts the car.

Compound Machines

Everyday tools often contain two or more simple machines. Tools that are made of a combination of simple machines are called compound machines. These pictures show some examples.

The scissors contain a pair of levers with the fulcrum in the middle. The cutting blades of the scissors are wedges.

Pedals on a bicycle are levers that attach to a system of connected wheels and axles. As the pedals turn, a chain in the wheel-and-axle system moves the big wheels on the bike.

A pair of scissors combines two simple machines: wedges and levers.

lever

effort

fulcrum

resistance

lever

wedges

wheel

wheels

A bicycle combines many simple machines, including levers and wheels and axles.

axle

lever

PROBLEM AND SOLUTION

What problems do machines solve?

3

What Forces Come from Magnets?

Magnetism comes from a special arrangement of an atom's electrons. Iron and many other metals are magnetic. Electric currents also create magnetic fields.

Magnets and Magnetic Fields

Prehistoric people discovered magnetism when they found magnetic rocks, called lodestones. Lodestones are mostly iron. They are able to attract or repel (push away) certain metals.

Today, we call this ability magnetism. It is a force created by the motion of electrons in atoms. Moving electrons produce magnetic fields. These are areas where a magnetic force can be observed. In some materials, electrons all line up in the same direction. When this happens, the magnetic fields around them combine. They create a strong magnet. Most magnets are metals, like iron, nickel, and cobalt.

MAGNETIC
The atoms of a magnet have tiny magnetic fields. They all point in the same direction. They combine to create a strong magnetic field.

NONMAGNETIC
The atoms of paper and other nonmagnetic materials have tiny magnetic fields. However, they point in all directions. They don't combine to make a strong magnet.

LIKE POLES REPEL
The iron filings show the attraction and repulsion of the magnets' magnetic fields. With the two north poles face to face, the magnets repel each other.

OPPOSITE POLES ATTRACT When opposite poles face each other, the magnets attract each other.

All the atoms face the same way in magnets. As a result, magnets have two specific regions, called poles. All magnets have a north pole at one end and a south pole at the other end.

Placing magnets end-to-end causes them to repel or attract each other. Place the same pole ends together, and magnets push each other away without even touching. Why? Their atoms point in opposite directions. Place opposite poles of two magnets together, and they attract. The atoms of both magnets all point the same direction. Their fields add together to make one big magnetic field.

A magnet shows if other materials are magnetic. If they are, the magnet "sticks" to them. For a time, the atoms in both objects line up the same way.

Atoms inside a magnet can be knocked out of line. Striking or heating a magnet may do this. For example, a magnet dropped on the floor will become weaker.

Making Magnets

Magnetic materials can become temporary magnets. A permanent magnet can be brought close to a magnetic material. This changes the alignment of atoms in the material. The alignment lasts as long as the material is near the magnet. In this way, the material itself can act as a magnet for a short time. Rubbing a magnet against an iron nail for a few minutes makes it a temporary magnet.

You can also pass magnetic material close to an electric current to make a magnet. Electrons moving through a wire create a magnetic field around the wire. If magnetic material is placed near the field, its atoms start to align. A magnet created this way is called an **electromagnet**.

The picture below shows an iron nail acting as an electromagnet.

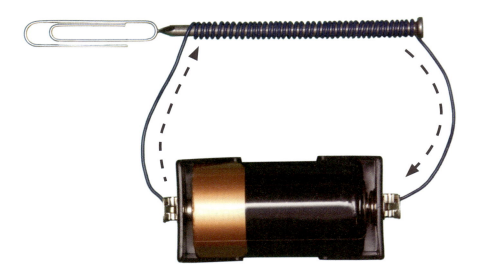

A battery sends electric current through a wire wrapped around a nail. The nail turns into an electromagnet. It attracts the paper clip.

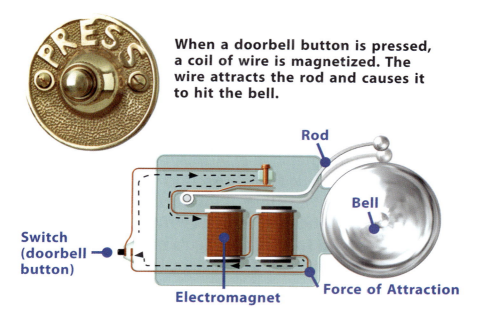

When a doorbell button is pressed, a coil of wire is magnetized. The wire attracts the rod and causes it to hit the bell.

Rod

Bell

Switch (doorbell button)

Electromagnet

Force of Attraction

How does the nail become an electromagnet? First, a piece of wire is wrapped around the nail. All the coils are wrapped in the same direction. Bare ends of the wire are connected to the battery. One end touches the positive terminal. One end touches the negative terminal. An electric current now runs through the wire. As long as it does, the nail acts like a magnet.

Wrapping more coils of wire around the magnet increases the strength of the electric current. This makes the electromagnet stronger, too. However, electric currents also give off heat. Too much current could heat the wire or the nail too much.

This battery setup will turn other magnetic materials into electromagnets, too. It would work on a paper clip, scissors, or a fork, for example.

Electromagnets have many uses. They can be powerful enough to pick cars up in the air! They also help run electric motors inside many household appliances.

Auroras

People who live far north see unusual red and green lights in the night sky at times. This is the aurora borealis (aw RAWR uh bawr ee AL ihs) or northern lights.

What causes the aurora? Earth is actually a magnet! It has a north magnetic pole and a south magnetic pole. It also has a magnetic field all around it. Magnetic lines of force are closest together at the magnetic poles.

Earth's magnetic field pulls electrons that shoot out from the Sun into space. The electrons zoom into Earth's upper atmosphere. They crash into atoms and molecules of gases that make up Earth's atmosphere. The electrons release energy during the crash, which leads to flashes of light. This is what people see as an aurora. The color of the aurora depends on the type of gas molecules that are hit by the electrons. Auroras, or southern lights, also happen near Earth's South Pole.

Aurora Borealis is Latin and means "dawn of the north."

DRAW CONCLUSIONS

What causes the atoms in an electromagnet to align?

Glossary

acceleration (ak sehl uh RAY shuhn), change in velocity

electromagnet (ih lehk troh MAG niht), a magnet that is powered by electricity

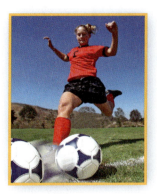

force (fawrs), push or pull acting on an object

friction (FRIHK shuhn), force from rubbing

gravity (GRAV ih tee), pulling force between objects

inertia (ih NUR shuh), resistance to a change in motion

Glossary

motion (MOH shuhn), change in an object's position

newton (NOOT n), unit to measure force, it is equal to the force required to accelerate a 1 kg mass by 1 m/s²

simple machine (SIHM puhl muh SHEEN), a machine that has few or no moving parts

speed (speed), measure of the distance an object moves in a given unit of time

velocity (vuh LAHS ih tee), measure of speed and direction

work (wurk), result of a force moving an object a certain distance

Responding

Think About What You Have Read

Vocabulary

❶ Air resistance is a form of _____.

A) gravity

B) magnetism

C) friction

D) velocity

Comprehension

❷ What are three ways an object may accelerate?

❸ Explain how three different simple machines other than inclined planes might be used to lift a heavy box.

❹ Suppose that two electromagnets attract each other, then suddenly repel each other. What conclusion could explain this observation?

Critical Thinking

❺ How are inclined planes and screws related? Describe ways they are used.

Energy and Waves

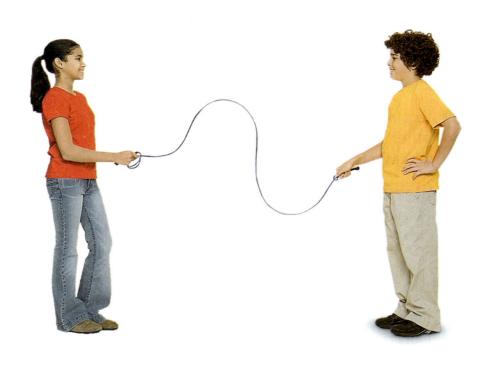

Contents

1

What Are Kinetic and Potential Energy?

Kinetic energy and potential energy can each be changed into the other. In all cases, energy is neither created nor destroyed.

Forms of Energy

Energy is the ability to do work. Energy and work are measured by the same unit, the joule.

Energy in its many forms shapes your life every day. For example, a lump of coal stores chemical energy. When coal burns, its chemical energy becomes light and heat. These are other forms of energy. When a fan spins, electrical energy from the motor becomes energy of the spinning parts. When a rock falls, its motion gives it energy.

Even objects at rest have energy. Remember that matter is made up of particles. The particles never stop moving. Their motion leads to thermal, or heat, energy. When energy changes form, some amount of it almost always is changed to heat.

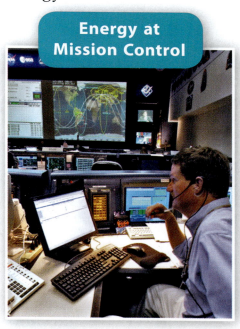

Energy at Mission Control

Electrical energy powers the computers. When controllers talk to astronauts, information passes over radio waves. This is a form of electromagnetic energy.

Visible light, including sunlight, is one type of electromagnetic energy. When Earth absorbs sunlight, electromagnetic energy turns into thermal energy. This warms Earth. Plants absorb sunlight, too. They make food, which they store as chemical energy.

A chemical reaction can release matter's chemical energy. Think back to the burning coal example. Likewise, chemical reactions in batteries help power flashlights.

Electricity is the movement of charged particles. People change electricity into other forms of energy every day. They use it to power toasters, TVs, computers, and many other things.

Energy at the Launch

Chemical energy in the rocket fuel becomes mechanical energy when the rocket lifts off. It also becomes thermal energy and electromagnetic energy.

Mechanical energy results from an object's motion or its position. For example, an acorn on a tree hangs above the ground. So, it has mechanical energy. When it falls, it has mechanical energy because it's moving.

Potential Energy and Kinetic Energy

Recall the definition of work. Work involves applying a force to matter over a distance. As work is done, energy either passes from one object to another or it changes form. In this way, work and energy are related. Energy is also related to matter and motion.

Kinetic energy is the energy of a moving object. **Potential energy** is energy that is stored in an object. Think of a bowler, for example. Chemical bonds in a bowler's muscles store potential energy that is used to throw the ball. Work is done when the ball starts rolling. The rolling ball has mechanical energy. When the ball hits a pin, more work is done. The ball's mechanical energy passes to the pin.

The charts show more examples of potential and kinetic energy.

Potential Energy

Potential Energy	Example
Chemical	battery
Elastic	compressed spring
Mechanical	rock on a ledge

Kinetic Energy

Kinetic Energy	Example
Sound	vibrating object
Thermal	hot cocoa
Mechanical	falling rock
Electrical	electrons in an electrical current

An archer is another example. In the picture, the archer uses energy to pull the bowstring. This bends the bow. The bow and the arrow have potential energy due to their position.

When the archer lets go of the bowstring, it unbends. This movement changes the bow's potential energy into kinetic energy. Some of that kinetic energy passes to the arrow. It flies forward.

Changing an object's shape can change its potential energy. So can changing an object's height.

Imagine lifting a box from the floor up to a table. You are applying a force to raise the box against the force of gravity. So, you do work on the box. As it rests on the table, the box has potential energy due to its height. What if the box falls off the table? Its potential energy becomes kinetic energy.

A pulled bow has potential energy. When the bow is released, the energy is changed to the kinetic energy of a moving bow and arrow.

Calculating Mechanical Energy

When an object that has potential mechanical energy starts moving, some of its potential energy turns into kinetic mechanical energy. As the object's kinetic energy increases, its potential energy decreases. Another way of saying this is that the mechanical energy (ME) of an object equals its potential energy (PE) plus its kinetic energy (KE).

$$ME = PE + KE$$

Look at the falling apple. At first, it is held up in the air by its stem. All of its mechanical energy is stored as potential energy, due to its height. The apple is not in motion. So, it has no kinetic energy.

All PE

Half PE   Half KE

All KE

In this time-lapse photograph, the energy of the falling apple changes from potential to kinetic.

Then the apple is dropped. As it starts to fall, it loses potential energy and gains kinetic energy. The farther the apple falls, the greater its kinetic energy and the less its potential energy. The total mechanical energy stays the same.

The instant before the apple hits the floor, all of its energy is kinetic energy. It will have no more potential energy relative to the ground.

A falling golf ball has converted all its potential mechanical energy to kinetic energy by the time it hits the water. This kinetic energy is transferred to the water, making waves.

CLASSIFY

Give two examples of energy changing from potential energy to kinetic energy.

2

How Are Sounds Made?

Sound is made by vibrations that transfer energy through air or other matter.

Mechanical Waves

A <mark>mechanical wave</mark> forms when a disturbance causes energy to travel through matter such as air or water. Mechanical waves can only move through matter. They cannot move through empty space. That's why you cannot hear sounds on the Moon.

Mechanical waves can move in different ways. In the picture, energy moves through a rope from left to right as the rope moves up and down. This is called a transverse wave. A transverse wave moves perpendicular to the direction that the medium moves. In the picture, the rope is the medium.

Part of the rope moves up as the energy moves through it. As that part drops back down, it sends energy to the next part of the rope. That part then moves up.

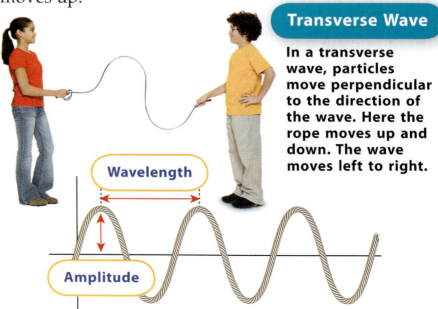

Transverse Wave

In a transverse wave, particles move perpendicular to the direction of the wave. Here the rope moves up and down. The wave moves left to right.

Wavelength

Amplitude

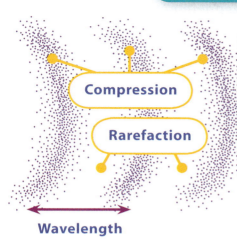

Compression

Rarefaction

Wavelength

In a longitudinal wave, particles move parallel to the direction the wave travels. They form compressions and rarefactions that move energy away from the source.

Mechanical waves can also move as longitudinal waves. Particles in the medium move back and forth parallel to the direction the wave travels. The picture here shows a spring snapping forward and back. Coils along the spring come together and spread apart as energy moves through them. The coils move back and forth only.

Compression happens wherever particles in a longitudinal wave come together. Rarefaction happens wherever particles spread out.

Scientists measure wave amplitude and wavelength. Amplitude is the height of the crests or troughs from the rest position of a transverse wave. Wavelength is the distance between two neighboring crests or troughs.

Scientists also measure wave frequency. This is the number of waves that pass a point per second. The shorter the wavelength, the higher the frequency. The longer the wavelength, the lower the frequency.

Sound Waves

Sound waves are a type of longitudinal mechanical wave. They move through air or other matter. Sound waves happen due to vibrations. A **vibration** is a rapid back-and-forth movement of an object.

Most sounds you hear carry through air. If you tap a pencil on your desk, both the pencil and the desk make tiny vibrations.

The vibrations compress and spread apart the air molecules around them. The first molecules to be pushed away bump into molecules next to them. These molecules then bump into other nearby molecules. At the same time, the first molecules return to their starting point.

In this way, sound waves spread out from the desk and the pencil like ripples in a pond. Sounds are short, because the pencil and desk do not vibrate for long.

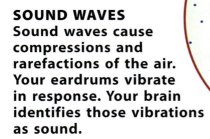

SOUND WAVES
Sound waves cause compressions and rarefactions of the air. Your eardrums vibrate in response. Your brain identifies those vibrations as sound.

Look at the sousaphone. The sousaphone makes sound when air travels through it. When the player's lips vibrate, the air inside the sousaphone vibrates, too. The vibrating air moves through the instrument. This makes the metal vibrate. The sound that comes out is magnified.

We can listen for sounds traveling through other mediums. Railroad workers will put their ears to the track to listen for oncoming trains. Woodpeckers listen to trees to hear the bugs inside them.

Waves travel at different speeds through different materials. This is true of all types of mechanical waves, including sound waves.

As a rule, sound waves move faster through solids and liquids than through gases. The temperature of the medium, especially gases, also affects the speed. The chart compares the speed of sound in different materials.

Speed of Sound in Different Materials

Material	Speed (m/s)
Dry air	346
Fresh water	1,500
Wood (oak)	1,850

Sousaphone

Pitch

Objects vibrate in different ways. So, they create sound waves with different properties. <mark>Pitch</mark> is how high or low you sense the sound to be.

Pitch depends on the sound wave's frequency. The higher the frequency of a wave, the higher the pitch of the sound.

Whistles make high-pitched sounds. This is because they vibrate at a high frequency. Sousaphones make low-pitched sounds. They vibrate at a low frequency.

A piano has many strings that vary in thickness and length. When you press a piano key, the sound you hear depends on which type of string starts to vibrate. Long, thick strings make low-pitched sounds. Short, thin strings make high-pitched sounds.

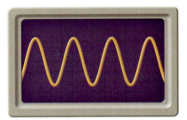

Low-frequency, loud sound

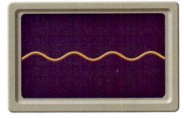

Low-frequency, soft sound

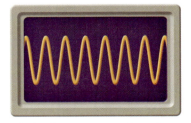

High-frequency, loud sound

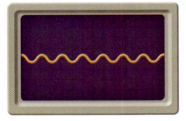

High-frequency, soft sound

SOUND WAVES
Digital recording software sets up graphs like these. They show sound waves moving as transverse waves. Amplitude shows volume. Frequency or wavelength shows pitch.

Decibel Levels of Common Sounds	
Sound	**Decibels**
Softest sound you can hear	1
Whisper	20
Normal speaking	60
Music through headphones	100
Thunder	120
Jet plane (from 30m)	140

Scientists measure the loudness of sound in units called decibels. Continuous sound above 85 decibels can cause hearing loss.

Volume

Volume is another property of sound. **Volume** is how loud or soft a sound is. It is a measure of the intensity, or strength, of the vibrations that lead to sound. The amplitude of the sound waves determines intensity.

For example, how loud or soft a guitar sounds depends on how forcefully you pluck its strings. Pluck a string lightly, and it will vibrate back and forth across a short distance. Air particles will be displaced a smaller distance from their rest positions. The string makes a soft sound.

Pluck harder, and the string will vibrate back and forth across a greater distance. Air particles will be displaced a greater distance from their rest positions. The string will make a louder sound. In both cases, the pitch stays the same.

Acoustics

Sound waves act in different ways when they move from one medium into another. When a sound wave strikes a surface, several things can happen. Sound may reflect off the surface. Sound may pass through it. Or the surface may absorb the sound. Acoustics is the study of how materials affect sound waves.

Imagine a sound wave in air hitting a concrete wall. Most of the sound wave will be reflected, or bounced off the wall. This is what happens when sound waves hit most hard, smooth surfaces. This is why you hear an echo when you yell into a canyon.

What happens when a sound wave hits a surface that is soft or has many tiny holes? Most of it will be absorbed. Cotton and other fabrics are examples of materials that are good at absorbing sounds.

This is one of the world's quietest rooms! The pyramid shapes help to prevent echoes. They also keep outside sounds from getting into the room.

Some materials reflect or absorb sound differently. This depends on the frequency of the sound. Builders keep this in mind when they plan music halls and theaters. They try to build a room that evens out sound frequencies that listeners hear.

What happens if a band plays in front of a wall that reflects mostly high-pitched frequencies? The music will sound thin and squeaky. What if the wall reflects mostly low-pitched frequencies? The music will sound dull. As a rule, back and side walls are made to absorb sound. If they were reflective, the music would not sound very clear.

This concert hall is designed to allow both the audience and the musicians on stage to hear the music clearly.

DRAW CONCLUSIONS

What is the difference between pitch and volume?

3

What Are Some Properties of Light?

Light waves are electromagnetic waves. Light can travel through a vacuum or through matter. White light can be separated into colors.

Electromagnetic Waves

Mechanical waves, such as sound waves, can only pass through matter, such as air or water. Electromagnetic waves can travel through a vacuum as well as matter. Electromagnetic waves include visible light, gamma rays, radio waves, microwaves, infrared rays, ultraviolet rays, and x-rays. The chart shows where these waves fall on the electromagnetic spectrum.

Different kinds of electromagnetic waves have different wavelengths and frequencies. Remember that wavelength is the distance between the wave's crests. Frequency is the number of wavelengths that pass a given point per second.

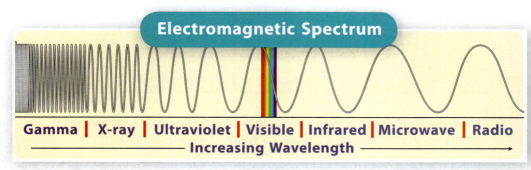

Electromagnetic Spectrum

Gamma | X-ray | Ultraviolet | Visible | Infrared | Microwave | Radio

Increasing Wavelength

Different types of electromagnetic radiation have different wavelengths and frequencies. As a result, they have different properties.

Visible light is radiation that people can see. It is in the middle of the spectrum. The picture shows how visible light can be split into colors.

The Sun and other stars give off all the wavelengths of electromagnetic waves. Some of these waves can harm living things. Luckily, Earth's atmosphere blocks many of them.

Different materials will reflect certain wavelengths of light and absorb others. The apple reflects red wavelengths. It absorbs other wavelengths.

Still, ultraviolet (UV) radiation in sunlight does reach Earth's surface. It is important to wear sunscreen outdoors to block UV radiation. Otherwise, it can cause skin cancer over time.

Electromagnetic waves interact differently with different materials. For example, radio waves can travel short distances through most materials. Visible light passes through transparent materials, such as glass. But most other materials block it.

A prism separates white light into different wavelengths of visible light. Wavelengths correspond to the colors you can see.

Reflection and Refraction

Electromagnetic waves act in different ways when they hit different materials. Sometimes the waves are absorbed. Absorbed light is changed into thermal energy. Other wavelengths may be reflected. **Reflection** takes place when a wave bounces off of a surface. Light reflecting from objects is what makes them visible.

A mirror is coated with metal that reflects almost all light that shines on it. When you look at a mirror, you see all the different wavelengths of light reflected. It is almost like looking at the object itself!

Light waves move at different speeds through different mediums. When light waves pass from one medium into another, they often change speed. As it changes speed, light refracts, or bends.

REFLECTION
A mirror reflects most of the light coming from an object. The image you see in the mirror looks very much like the object itself—you!

REFRACTION
Refraction causes the pencil to appear broken, even though it is not.

Refraction takes place when the path of a light wave changes as it moves from one medium to another.

For example, look at the picture of the pencil in the glass. The pencil appears to be broken, but it is not. Light is traveling at different speeds through each medium: water, glass, and air. The light waves refract, or bend, as they pass through each medium before reaching the lens of the camera snapping the picture. This is what makes the pencil look like it is broken.

How can refraction be put to good use? Tools that refract light include eyeglasses, contact lenses, cameras, microscopes, and telescopes.

All of these tools use lenses. A **lens** is a curved piece of clear material that refracts light in a controlled way. Lenses are typically glass or plastic. They can refract light to create useful images of an object.

There are many kinds of lenses. A convex lens is thicker at the center than at its edges. This type of lens bends light rays toward one another.

A concave lens is thinner at its center. It bends light rays away from one another.

Your eyes have lenses to help them see. In an eye with perfect vision, the lens focuses images onto a structure called the retina.

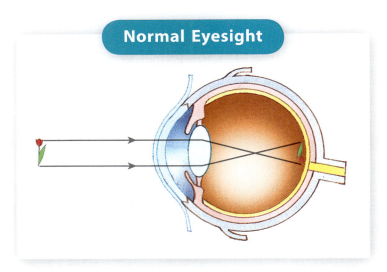

Normal Eyesight

Light that passes through the lens of the eye is refracted. As a result, it focuses an image at the back of the eye, or retina.

Sometimes, images form just a bit in front of or behind the retina. When this happens, vision is blurry. Corrective lenses can fix the problem. Glasses and contact lenses are corrective lenses. They bend light rays just enough to focus the image correctly.

By combining convex and concave lenses in different ways, people can make many different tools. For example, many telescopes use two convex lenses to make faraway objects look larger. Microscopes use lenses to make small objects appear larger.

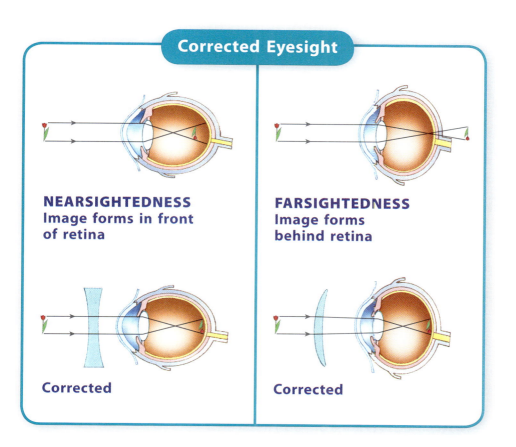

Corrected Eyesight

NEARSIGHTEDNESS
Image forms in front of retina

FARSIGHTEDNESS
Image forms behind retina

Corrected

Corrected

Fiber Optics

Reflection of light makes the use of fiber optics possible. In fiber optics, special fibers carry light waves along a cable that bends.

Optical fibers

Fiber optics has made it easier to communicate over telephones and the Internet. It has made it easier for a doctor to look down a patient's throat and into the stomach.

Remember that light travels in a straight line as a rule. How can it follow the looping path of an optical fiber?

Optical fibers are lined with a special coating that reflects light. Light waves reflect off the inside of the fiber nonstop as they move through it. They strike at very wide angles. This causes light waves to reflect off the coating instead of passing through it. The light acts just as if it is hitting a mirror. This is called total internal reflection. It allows fibers to send light over long distances.

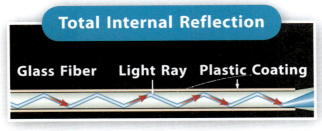

Total Internal Reflection

Glass Fiber   Light Ray   Plastic Coating

Total internal reflection causes light waves to reflect off the coating instead of passing through it.

CAUSE AND EFFECT

What property of light is used in optical fibers?

Glossary

energy (EHN uhr jee), ability to do work

kinetic energy (kih NEHT ihk EHN uhr jee), energy of a moving object

lens (lehnz), curved piece of clear material that refracts light in a predictable way

mechanical wave (mih KAN ih kuhl wayv), wave that can travel only through matter

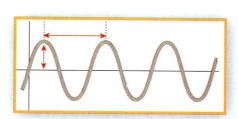

pitch (pihch), perceived highness or lowness of a sound

potential energy (puh TEHN shuhl EHN uhr jee), energy stored in an object

Glossary

reflection (rih FLEHK shuhn), bouncing of a wave off a material

refraction (rih FRAK shuhn), changing of the path of a wave as it moves between materials of different densities

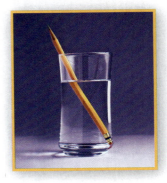

vibration (vy BRAY shuhn), rapid back-and-forth movement

visible light (VIHZ uh buhl lyt), portion of the electro-magnetic spectrum humans can see

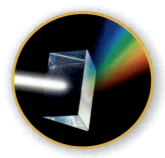

volume (VAHL yoom), loudness of a sound, or the space an object takes up

Think About What You Have Read

Vocabulary

❶ An example of kinetic energy is _____ .

A) a rock held above the ground

B) a bowstring pulled back

C) a barrel of oil

D) a moving roller coaster

Comprehension

❷ What is the difference between potential energy and kinetic energy?

❸ What are sound waves and how do they travel?

❹ What causes light to refract? Give an example from everyday life.

Critical Thinking

❺ How might you improve the sound quality in a music hall where the music sounds high-pitched and squeaky?

Temperature and Heat

Contents

What Is Thermal Energy?

Thermal energy is the total kinetic energy of the particles that make up a substance.

Temperature and Thermal Energy

All matter is made up of tiny particles, such as atoms and molecules. These particles are always moving. This means they have kinetic energy. **Thermal energy** is the total kinetic energy of the particles within a material.

Each cup below holds the same amount of soup. But the cup of hot soup has much more thermal energy. Why? The particles of the hot soup move faster than the particles of the cold soup. Faster particles have more kinetic energy.

We use words such as hot and cold to talk about temperature. **Temperature** is a measure of the average kinetic energy of particles within a material. The hot soup has a higher temperature. Its particles have a greater kinetic energy.

Comparing Thermal Energy

COLD SOUP Slow-moving particles have little kinetic energy.

HOT SOUP Fast-moving particles have lots of kinetic energy.

Thermometers have temperature scales. Units on the scale are called degrees. The degree symbol is a small raised circle. Most people measure temperature with the Fahrenheit scale or the Celsius scale.

People in the United States prefer the Fahrenheit scale. In the picture, this scale appears on the right side of the thermometer.

The Celsius scale is more commonly used in science and by people around the world. In the picture, it appears on the left side of the thermometer. Notice that water freezes at 32°F or 0°C. Water boils at 212°F or 100°C.

Many thermometers have a thin glass tube. The tube holds a liquid, often mercury or alcohol. As temperatures rise and fall, the liquid does, too. This is because the liquid expands when thermal heat is added. It contracts as thermal heat is removed.

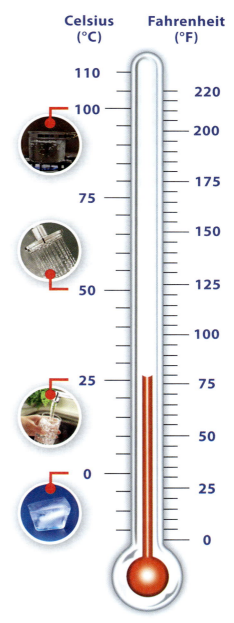

TEMPERATURE Water's characteristics change with temperature. What is water like at 23°C?

Heat

Thermal energy is often made when other forms of energy go through a change. This is what happens when solar energy from the Sun strikes an object and warms it. Other sources of thermal energy include chemical reactions, friction, and electricity.

Look at the large urn of hot cocoa in the picture. Cocoa from the urn was just poured into the cup. The cocoa in the cup has the same temperature as the cocoa in the urn.

However, the urn contains more cocoa. This means it has more particles in motion. So, it has more thermal energy than the cocoa in the cup. Cocoa in the cup, having less thermal energy, will cool faster.

Thermal energy can move through matter. The movement of thermal energy from warmer parts of matter to cooler parts is called **heat**.

30 cups

1 cup

The large urn and the small cup hold cocoa that is at the same temperature. But the cocoa in the urn has 30 times more thermal energy.

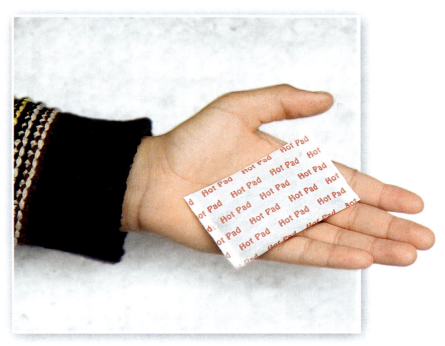

What makes a hand warmer heat up? Its thermal energy comes from an electrical battery or from the reaction of chemicals in the warmer.

An empty cup feels cool to the touch. Fill it with hot liquid, and it feels warm. That change in temperature is a result of the transfer of thermal energy. The transfer happens when hot liquid particles crash into cooler particles in the cup. The average kinetic energy of the particles of the cup increases. The cup gets warmer. The liquid loses some thermal energy. It gets cooler.

Heat does not just pass from the liquid to the cup. It can travel to all matter the cup touches. Think of the cocoa example again. In time, the liquid, the cup, the air, and the part of the tabletop touching the cup will all have the same temperature.

Thermal energy always passes from warmer matter to cooler matter. In the picture below, the snowball has a lower temperature than the boy's hand. So, thermal energy moves from the hand to the snowball. The hand gets cold because it loses thermal energy. Cold does not pass from the snowball to the hand.

The pretzel in the other hand is warm. Thermal energy spreads to the boy's hand. The hand becomes warmer. As the pretzel loses thermal energy, it cools. Its temperature approaches the temperature of the boy's hand and the air.

SNOW The snowball is colder than the boy's hand. Thermal energy moves from the hand to the snow. The snowball gets warmer. It starts to melt.

HOT PRETZEL The pretzel is warmer than the boy's hand. So, thermal energy moves from the pretzel to the hand. The hand gets warm. The pretzel cools.

Specific Heat Capacity

Different materials heat up at different rates. Look at the picture below. Both the water and the concrete walkway have received the same amount of sunlight for the same amount of time. But the water is much cooler than the concrete. You will feel this if you walk across the concrete and jump in the pool.

If conditions are the same, why are the temperatures different? Part of this is due to different specific heat capacities. Specific heat capacity is the amount of thermal energy needed to raise 1 g of a given material by 1°C. The chart below shows the specific heat capacities for some common materials.

Substance	Specific Heat Capacity
water	4.18
ice	2.05
concrete	0.88

MAIN IDEA

What is temperature?

2 How Does Thermal Energy Spread?

Thermal energy is transferred by conduction, convection, and radiation.

Conduction

Thermal energy is spread, or transferred, one of three ways. These are conduction, convection, and radiation. Transfer of thermal energy through direct contact is called **conduction**.

Conduction happens mainly in solids. Rapidly vibrating particles move in a back-and-forth motion. They bump into nearby particles as a result. In doing so, they pass some of their kinetic energy to these particles. This causes the other particles to vibrate more rapidly. This is how thermal energy spreads throughout a solid object. This also is how it spreads among solid objects that are touching.

The picture below shows conduction at work. The pan sits on a hot burner. So, thermal energy from the burner spreads to the bottom of the pan. In turn, the pan transfers heat to the food.

CONDUCTION Through conduction, thermal energy passes from the burner to the pan.

Heater

CONVECTION Currents of water or air created by the process of convection are called convection currents.

Convection

Solids are rigid, but liquids and gases are not. Their particles can move much more freely. The temperature of a gas or liquid rises when a hot object touches it. The gas or liquid expands and becomes less dense. Warm, light liquids will rise. Cold, dense liquids will sink. This process is called **convection**. It is how thermal energy spreads through liquids and gases.

The fish tank above has a heater. The heater warms water that flows around it. Warm water expands and rises. It takes thermal energy with it. It loses some of that energy every time warm and cold water particles bump into each other.

At the surface, the warm water loses more thermal energy. The energy spreads to the surrounding water and the air. The water cools and becomes denser. It sinks and is heated again.

Radiation

Thermal energy can also be transferred by **radiation**. Radiation is the transfer of energy by electromagnetic waves. All objects emit, or give off, thermal radiation. Even ice caps at the North Pole emit a little. Living things, including your body, emit some radiation. A hot burner on a stove emits much more.

When an object absorbs thermal radiation, its particles vibrate faster. This increases their kinetic energy. Their temperature rises.

The most important source of radiation for Earth is the Sun. The Sun emits radiation of different wavelengths. Some are waves of visible light. Others are infrared (ihn fruh REHD) light. They have a longer wavelength. Infrared radiation gives the Sun most of its heating power. We depend on the Sun for light and heat. Likewise, a campfire radiates helpful light and heat.

RADIATION The fire emits infrared waves. The waves radiate in all directions. This warms the campers.

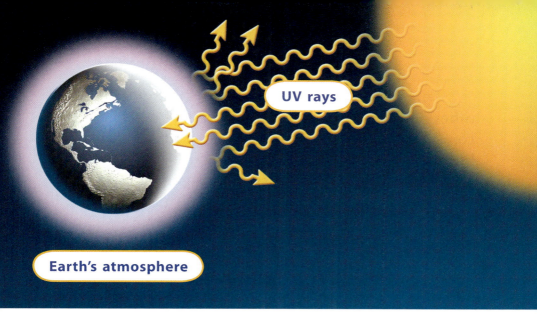

UV rays

Earth's atmosphere

Earth's atmosphere blocks some of the harmful UV rays from the Sun.

Infrared radiation affects the motions of the particles of your body. Longer infrared wavelengths greatly increase the speed of particles in your body. You feel heat. Shorter infrared wavelengths increase particle movement very little. You do not feel heat as a result.

All electromagnetic waves carry energy. Objects that absorb these waves also receive some of their thermal energy.

This explains why light-colored clothes help keep you cool on hot days. Their colors reflect more solar radiation than they absorb. In contrast, darker colors absorb more solar radiation than they reflect. Wear them on cold, sunny days to keep warmer.

Ultraviolet (UV) rays have shorter wavelengths than visible light. Earth's upper atmosphere blocks some, but not all, UV rays. If your skin absorbs too much UV radiation, you get sunburned. You should wear sunscreen. It blocks UV rays.

Conductors and Insulators

Some materials transfer thermal energy better than other materials. This kind of material is called a **conductor**. Most solids are better conductors than liquids or gases. The particles in solids are close together. So, vibrations pass more easily among them.

Most metals are excellent heat conductors. Other solids, such as wood, conduct heat much more slowly. These solids contain "pockets" of air trapped between their particles. Vibrations do not transfer as easily.

Look at the picture. The boiling water passes its thermal energy to the spoons by the process of conduction. The metal spoon on the right will grow too hot to touch. The wooden spoon will stay cool enough to handle.

Likewise, a plastic spoon would not pick up a lot of heat from boiling water. Wood and plastic are insulators. An **insulator** is a material that is a poor conductor of heat.

The metal spoon transfers thermal energy better than the wooden spoon. Metal is a better conductor than wood.

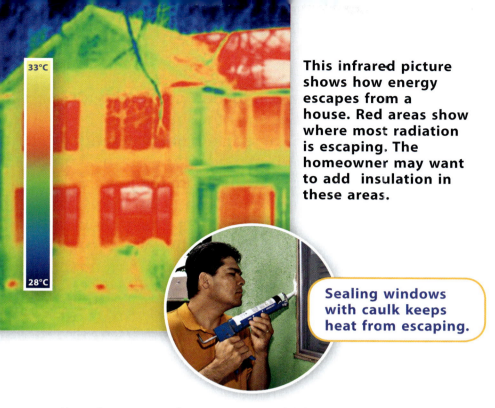

This infrared picture shows how energy escapes from a house. Red areas show where most radiation is escaping. The homeowner may want to add insulation in these areas.

Sealing windows with caulk keeps heat from escaping.

Insulators, such as coats and blankets, trap the thermal energy that your body makes. This helps keep you warm. The thermal energy cannot escape into the air. Remember: thermal energy is transferred from warmer regions to colder regions.

Houses and buildings are also designed with heat transfer in mind. In cold-weather areas, house walls are lined with pockets of non-moving air. The pockets act as insulation. They keep heat from leaving the house.

Fiberglass insulation traps heat even better than air. And it really cuts down on energy costs. Homeowners can install it and save hundreds of dollars each year.

Glass windows help to heat homes by transmitting radiant energy. Glass allows sunlight to pass through into your house. This thermal energy stays inside, because glass is a fairly poor conductor.

Home Heating

Heating systems use conduction, convection, or radiation to warm homes and other buildings.

For example, in a metal radiator, hot water pumps through the radiator's rib-like sides. The ribs heat up as a result. Then they radiate heat into the room.

Forced air heaters use convection. A fan forces heated air through pipes called ducts. Ducts blow warm air into each room in the building.

The baseboard heater in the picture uses all three methods of heat transfer.

First, electricity passes through the heater. Convection transfers electrical heat to long rows of thin metal pieces. These pieces are called vanes. Heat radiates from the vanes into air spaces between them. This air expands as it warms. It flows out the open front of the baseboard. The baseboard keeps pulling air from the room to warm it, release it, and warm it again.

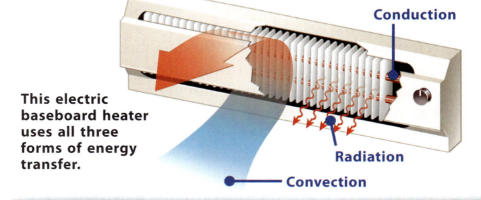

Conduction

This electric baseboard heater uses all three forms of energy transfer.

Radiation

Convection

MAIN IDEA

How do conduction and convection compare?

Glossary

conduction (kuhn DUHK shuhn), transfer of thermal energy between two substances or between two parts of the same substance

conductor (kuhn DUHK tuhr), material that easily transfers thermal energy or electricity

convection (kuhn VEHK shuhn), transfer of thermal energy by the flow of liquids or gases

heat (heet), transfer of thermal energy from warmer areas to cooler areas

insulator (IHN suh lay tuhr), material that does not easily transfer thermal energy or electricity

Glossary

radiation (ray dee AY shuhn), transfer of thermal energy through electromagnetic waves

temperature (TEHM puhr uh chur), measure of the average kinetic energy of the particles that make up a substance

thermal energy (THUHR muhl EHN uhr jee), total kinetic energy of the particles of a substance

Think About What You Have Read

Vocabulary

❶ Thermal energy is often transferred in gases and liquids by _____.

A) convection

B) conduction

C) radiation

C) electromagnetic waves

Comprehension

❷ What is thermal energy? Describe two objects that have different thermal energy.

❸ What kinds of infrared waves are felt as heat?

❹ Name and describe three ways that thermal energy is transferred.

Critical Thinking

❺ How would you decide if a material would make a good conductor? Describe a test you might perform.

Electrical Energy

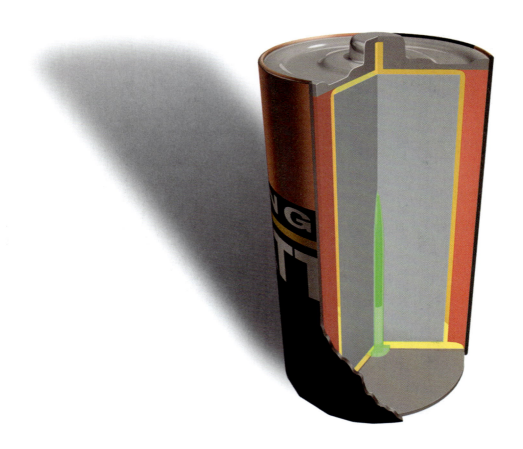

Contents

1

How Is Electricity Produced?

Electricity is the movement of electrons from one place to another. It can be produced by transforming, or changing, other forms of energy.

Static and Current Electricity

Have you ever rubbed a balloon on a carpet, then placed it against a wall? The balloon might stay on the wall for a minute or longer! Static electricity is the reason why. **Static electricity** is an electric force between non-moving electric charges.

To set up the balloon trick, you must rub a balloon against certain kinds of carpet. Electrons from the carpet jump to the balloon. The balloon now has extra electrons. So, it takes on an overall negative charge. The opposite happens if you rub a balloon against plastic. Electrons jump off the balloon. The balloon now has fewer electrons. So, it has an overall positive charge.

Rubbing helps electrons move from the carpet to the blue balloons. They gain a negative charge. Electrons move from the orange balloon to the plastic. The orange balloon takes on a positive charge.

Charged objects apply a force on one another. Two objects with the same charges repel, or push away from each other. Two objects with opposite charges attract, or pull toward each other.

Look at the pictures of the balloons. The blue pair repels each other. Both balloons have a negative charge. The blue and orange pair pulls together. They have opposite charges.

Have you ever walked across a thick carpet, then touched a metal doorknob? You might have felt a mild shock! You might have even seen a spark. Static electricity was being discharged, or released. Electrons moved between you and the doorknob. Lightning is a great big spark of static electricity! It has a lot of energy. But it lasts a very short time.

Charge Behavior

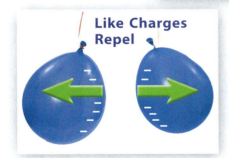

The two negatively charged balloons repel each other.

The negatively and positively charged balloons attract each other.

Batteries and Fuel Cells

A battery contains one or more electrochemical cells. The cells use chemical reactions to create an <mark>electric current</mark>. An electric current is an unbroken flow of electric charge through a pathway.

Look at the battery in the picture. It is made with manganese dioxide, powdered zinc, and a paste called an electrolyte (ih LEHK truh lyt). Imagine wiring the battery to a light bulb. Electric current flows as chemical reactions start happening. Zinc loses electrons. The electrons move through the brass nail. They exit the negative terminal. The electrons flow through the wires and light bulb. Then they return through the positive terminal. Manganese dioxide picks them up.

ALKALINE BATTERY
Alkali is another name for a base. A base is the opposite of an acid. Alkaline batteries use a base as an electrolyte.

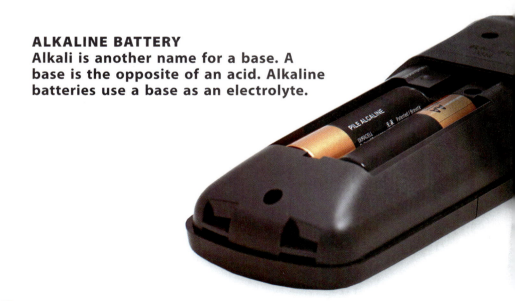

In time, either the zinc or the electrolyte will be used up. The chemical reactions will stop, and so will the current.

Take used batteries to a battery-recycling center. The chemicals in batteries can poison people. They can also poison soil and water if they leak.

People use many kinds of batteries. Car batteries can be recharged and used again and again.

In the future, fuel cells may be used in place of some batteries. Fuel cells also use chemical reactions. They mix oxygen and hydrogen gases. Water is given off. So is an electric current. Fuel cells run for as long as they have enough fuel. Right now, we don't have hydrogen stations for hydrogen cars. But fuel cells have been used in space since the 1960s.

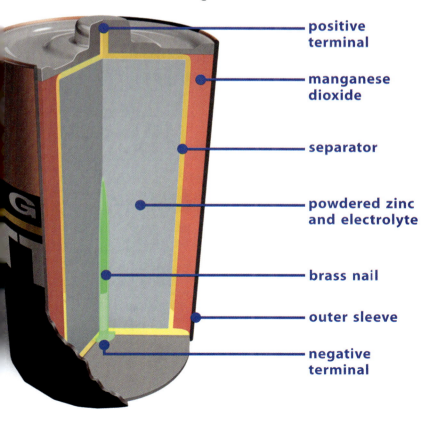

positive terminal

manganese dioxide

separator

powdered zinc and electrolyte

brass nail

outer sleeve

negative terminal

Making Electricity

What makes the electricity that powers your home and school? The answer is an electric generator. An **electric generator** is a machine that changes mechanical kinetic energy to electrical energy. Look at the picture of the bicycle light. The light is powered by a friction generator. How? The spinning wheel passes some of its mechanical kinetic energy to the generator. The generator turns it into electrical energy.

How does an electric generator produce an electric current? A loop of wire turns at great speed inside the generator. It moves through a magnetic field. This produces an electric current in the wire.

generator

The bicycle light is powered by a generator. The turning bicycle wheel turns the toothed wheel on the generator. This produces mechanical energy for the generator.

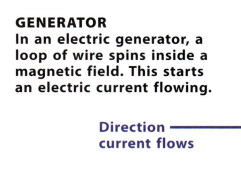

Direction wire turns

GENERATOR
In an electric generator, a loop of wire spins inside a magnetic field. This starts an electric current flowing.

Direction current flows

magnets

N   S

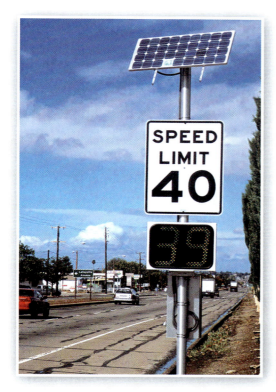

SOLAR CELLS
Some roadside signs are powered by solar cells.

What turns the loop of wire? The mechanical energy to turn the wire can come from many sources. As you saw, it could come from a spinning bike wheel. Electric power plants need much bigger energy sources. They may burn fossil fuels to get energy needed to turn the wires. Or they may catch the power of moving water and wind. They may even split atoms! You will read more about power plants on the next page.

Solar cells can also produce electricity. Solar cells are made of semiconductors, such as silicon. Sunlight strikes the cell and knocks electrons out of silicon atoms. An electric current starts to flow.

Electric Power Plants

The electricity that powers your home comes from a power plant. Almost all power plants use the same kind of electric generators. Energy to run the generators may come from different sources.

Many power plants burn coal or other fossil fuels. As coal burns, its energy heats water, which turns to steam. The steam turns turbines, which are like large fans. The spinning turbines run the electric generators.

Hydroelectric power plants use running water to turn turbines. These plants are built on rivers, near dams. The dams direct the water into the turbines.

Like coal-burning plants, nuclear power plants use steam to turn turbines. However, they get energy from splitting atoms, not coal! Uranium is used for this splitting process, called nuclear fission.

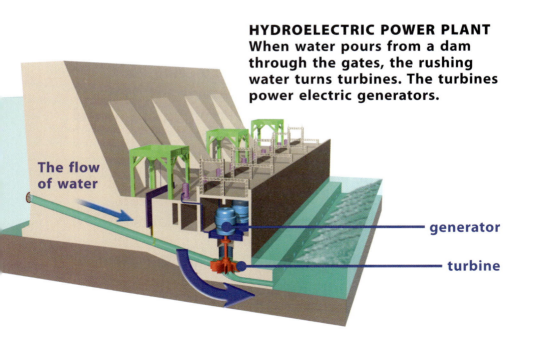

HYDROELECTRIC POWER PLANT
When water pours from a dam through the gates, the rushing water turns turbines. The turbines power electric generators.

The flow of water

generator

turbine

We now know these energy sources have some drawbacks. Fossil fuels are running out. Plus, burning them can pollute the environment. Hydroelectric dams can hurt ecosystems around them. Used fuel from nuclear power plants is dangerous. It is hard to get rid of safely.

Scientists are working on cleaner, safer sources of energy. For example, windmills catch wind energy. Solar cells and panels use the Sun's energy. Geothermal power makes use of heat from Earth's interior. These energy sources are not in widespread use yet. With the right equipment and funding, that could change.

TEXT STRUCTURE

What supplies the kinetic energy to a hydroelectric power plant?

Hydroelectric dams can hurt river systems where they operate.

2

What Is an Electric Circuit?

An electric circuit is a pathway for electrons to travel. The energy of moving electrons can be changed into different forms, including light, heat, and sound.

Circuits

A circuit is a closed loop. An object in a circuit begins at a starting point. It moves through the loop until it gets back to the start. It does not backtrack at any time. Think about a water park ride. Boats start at the high point of the track. Water carries them down a path. Then boats travel back to the high point to pick up new riders. What would happen if part of the path was missing or blocked off? Or what if the motor that lifted the boats stopped working? The ride would stop. The boats could not finish their circuit.

This roller coaster ride is a circuit.
A circuit is a closed loop.

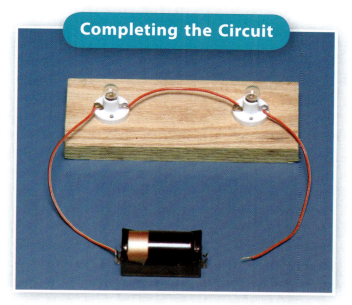

The battery cannot light the bulbs. The circuit has not been completed. When the wire is touched to the other end of the battery, the circuit will be complete. Electric current will flow to light the bulbs.

The path for an electric current is called an <mark>electric circuit</mark>. The electric charges are like the boats in the ride. The battery in the circuit is like the motor that lifts the boats to the top of the track. The motor does work to lift each boat. It gives them higher gravitational potential energy. The battery does work to "lift" each charge. Charges are given higher electric potential energy. <mark>Voltage</mark> is a measure of a battery's lifting force. It measures the amount of electric potential energy per unit charge.

Like the boats in the ride, electric current follows a set path. Conductors and insulators are materials that affect the path a current can take.

A **conductor** is a material that carries electricity well. Most wires used in electric circuits are made of copper. This metal is a very good conductor. Other metals make good conductors, too.

An **insulator** is a material that does not carry electricity very well. Plastic is a good insulator. Most wires are coated with plastic for this reason. Wood and air are also good insulators.

Do you think water is a better conductor or insulator? If you chose conductor, you are right. Electricity passes very easily through water. You should keep electric machines away from water. If they get wet, you could get an electric shock.

A circuit may be closed or open. In a closed circuit, electric current passes through the conductor again and again. In an open circuit, insulators block the path of the current. The current stops.

When plugged in, a string of party lights is a closed circuit.

The arrows show the direction of the current through a closed circuit. If the switch opens, an open circuit is created. The current stops.

A **switch** can open or close a circuit. A switch is a simple part that moves. As it moves, it opens or closes a path for electricity.

Look closely at the electric circuit here. When the switch is closed, the circuit is closed. The electric current flows all the way around the circuit. On its way, it lights the bulb. The arrows show which way the current moves.

Series Circuit

Look at the picture. Batteries, wires, and light bulbs make up a closed circuit. Electricity takes a single path through the circuit. If you cut a wire or remove a bulb, you open the whole circuit. The same is true if a bulb burns out.

This picture shows a **series circuit**. In a series circuit, electricity follows just one path. It flows between two or more light bulbs or other pieces of equipment. You can add bulbs. But they will be less bright. All the bulbs must share voltage from the battery.

The picture also shows a diagram, or drawing, of the circuit. Zigzag lines stand for light bulbs, which are resistors. Long and short dashes stand for the battery.

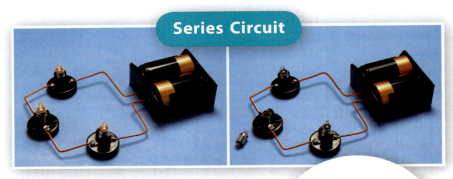

Series Circuit

These three light bulbs are part of a series circuit. Remove one bulb and the others go out. The circuit was opened. The diagram shows the same circuit. People who work with circuits use diagrams like these.

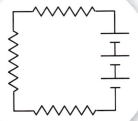

Parallel Circuit

The picture here shows the same battery and three light bulbs. However, their order is different. Electricity takes a different path to reach each bulb.

This is called a parallel circuit. In a **parallel circuit**, electric current can follow two or more different paths.

When you take a bulb away, you only open that bulb's path. The other bulbs stay lit!

In a parallel circuit, light bulbs do not share voltage from the battery. Each bulb is as bright as if it were the only bulb in the circuit.

The circuits in your home are set up in parallel series. If you turn off a lamp, other lights stay on. So does anything else that is plugged into the circuit.

Parallel Circuit

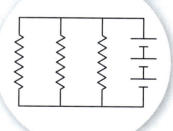

These three bulbs are wired in a parallel circuit. Remove one light bulb, and only one part of the circuit becomes open. The other bulbs stay lit.

Electrical Safety

Be safe around electricity. Only plug electrical equipment into household outlets. Otherwise, you could get shocked!

Electricity can also produce heat as a side effect. Lamps and other equipment can overheat. So can electric wires. Fires can even start this way. The higher the current, the stronger the heat.

Fuses and circuit breakers can stop circuits from overheating. Most homes use them.

A fuse has a thin metal strip inside it. The strip is part of an electric circuit. The strip will melt if the current flowing to it gets too high. When this happens, the circuit opens.

A circuit breaker works a lot like a fuse. A circuit breaker has a switch in place of a metal strip. Too much current trips the switch. The circuit opens. You can close the circuit by flipping the switch back closed.

So, circuit breakers can be used again and again. Fuses must be replaced after they stop electricity just once. For this reason, most new homes use circuit breakers.

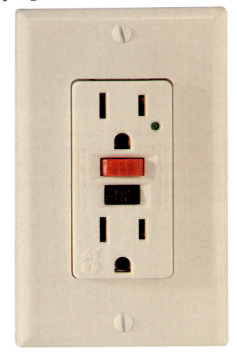

This wall outlet has a red button that connects to a certain kind of circuit breaker. The button pops out to break the circuit. This keeps you from getting an electric shock.

Tongue

The tongue inside a fuse melts if current is too high. This breaks the circuit. A new fuse has to be put in to close the circuit.

Circuit breakers throw a switch when current gets too high. Circuit breakers can be used over and over again.

DRAW CONCLUSIONS

How do series circuits and parallel circuits differ?

3

How Do People Use Electricity?

Electrical energy is turned into light, mechanical energy, and thermal energy for many everyday uses.

Energy Transformations

Electrical energy powers many of the tools we use every day. We can plug a machine into a wall to tap into electricity. We can put batteries in equipment to create electric current. Electric energy changes form as we operate these machines and equipment.

For example, the man in the picture wears a headlamp. The headlamp uses a simple series circuit. The circuit includes a battery, a switch, and a light bulb. The light bulb has a thread-like wire called a filament. The filament resists, or works against, the flow of current. As a result, it heats up and gives off light. Electrical energy becomes light and thermal energy.

RADIANT ENERGY
Electrical energy changes inside a headlamp. It becomes light. Light is a form of radiant energy.

The hair dryer also uses electricity to make heat. Thin wire is coiled inside the hair dryer. The wire resists the electric current with great force. As a result, the wires heat up. Air inside the hair dryer heats up, too.

A fan in the hair dryer turns electrical energy into mechanical kinetic energy. The hot air blows out. Switches control airflow and temperature.

The saw also turns electrical energy into mechanical kinetic energy. It has a switch to control speed. A person presses the switch lightly to keep a low speed. Less current flows and the motor runs slower. A person presses the switch all the way to go full speed.

MECHANICAL ENERGY
Electrical energy changes inside a saw. It becomes mechanical kinetic energy that runs a motor.

THERMAL ENERGY
Electrical energy changes inside a hair dryer. It becomes thermal energy as metal coils heat up.

Electric Motors

An **electric motor** changes electrical energy into mechanical kinetic energy. To do this, a motor uses both an electromagnet and a permanent magnet. The motor is built so that the poles of the electromagnet keep switching positions. This keeps the motor spinning.

A DC motor runs on direct current (DC) only. You can see the parts of a DC motor in the drawing. Here is how they work:

A frame called an armature spins around an axle inside two magnets. The armature has a rod wrapped with wire coils. The coils connect to a commutator. The commutator also touches brushes that are wired to the power supply. The brushes are springy metal pieces that "brush" against the commutator. When the motor is on, current passes through all these parts.

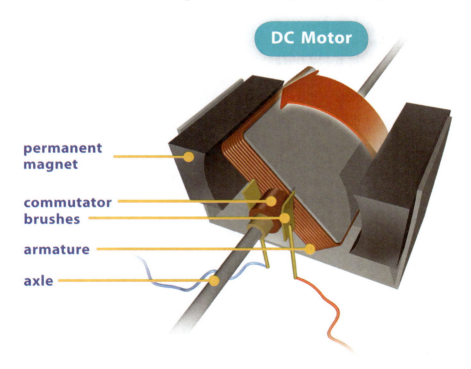

DC Motor

permanent magnet

commutator

brushes

armature

axle

The current makes the armature act like an electromagnet. The armature starts to spin as it is pushed away by the permanent magnet. The magnets' like poles repel each other. Normally, the armature would spin all the way around. The opposite poles of the magnets would come together. The poles would attract. The armature would stop spinning, and the motor would stop working.

Just as this is about to happen, the circuit gets broken. The armature stops acting like an electromagnet for a very short time. Then current begins flowing again. But now, it runs in the other direction. This reverses the poles of the electromagnet. So, the armature makes a half-spin the other way. This all happens at high speed.

Different motors drive each set of wheels. This allows the wheelchair to turn or move straight.

Power Distribution

You know that electricity for your house comes from a power plant. The power plant may be far from where you live.

Electric power comes to your house through wires. Some of this power may be lost as heat along the way. Power companies do not want this to happen. Less electricity is lost if it is sent at high voltages. So power companies increase the voltage of electricity leaving the plant. They use equipment called a step-up transformer. A step-down transformer lowers voltage. This happens just before electricity reaches your home. Your home gets just the voltage it needs to run most things in your house.

Wires are placed high above the ground for safety. High voltages can badly hurt people.

CAUSE AND EFFECT

Why does a light bulb filament glow?

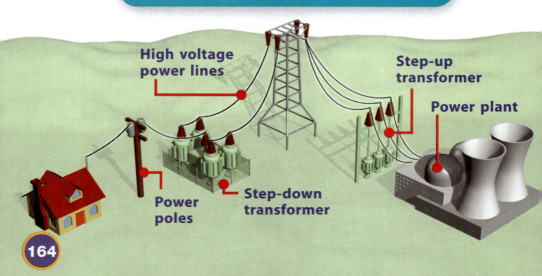

How Electricity Reaches Your Home

High voltage power lines

Step-up transformer

Power plant

Power poles

Step-down transformer

Glossary

conductor (kuhn DUHK tuhr), material that easily transfers thermal energy or electricity

electric circuit (ih LEHK trihk SUR kiht), pathway for an electric current

electric current (ih LEHK trihk KUR uhnt), continuous flow of electric charge along a pathway

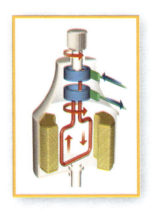

electric generator (ih LEHK trihk JEHN uh ray tuhr), device that converts kinetic energy to electricity

electric motor (ih LEHK trihk MOH tuhr), device that converts electrical energy into kinetic energy

insulator (IHN suh lay tuhr), material that does not easily transfer thermal energy or electricity

Glossary

parallel circuit (PAR uh leh SUR kiht), circuit where electric current can follow two or more different paths

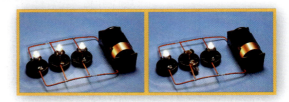

series circuit (SIHR eez SUR kiht), circuit where only a single path for electricity connects two or more devices

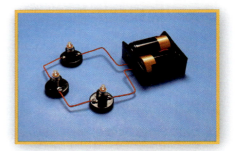

static electricity (STAT ihk ih lehk TRIHS ih tee), electrical force between nonmoving electric charges

switch (swihch), movable section of a circuit that can open or close a path for electricity

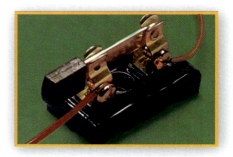

voltage (VOHL tihj), measure of the force that moves electrons

Responding

Think About What You Have Read

Vocabulary

1. A ________ is a device that breaks a circuit when the current becomes too high.

   A) fuse

   B) switch

   C) wire

   D) transformer

Comprehension

2. What is electric current?

3. Why does an electric circuit have to be closed for it to work?

4. What are two ways that electrical energy is changed to other forms of energy?

Critical Thinking

5. Are fuses a necessary part of a household electric circuit? What might work better? Explain.

Using Resources Wisely

Contents

How Do People Use Resources?

Earth provides many resources, or useful things, that people need. Some resources are found only in small amounts. Other resources seem like they may never run out.

Natural Resources

The natural world gives us everything that we need to stay alive, and many things that we find useful or helpful. These resources include air, water, minerals, and soil. They are called **natural resources**.

People have found many ways to use natural resources. We use them to build houses, grow crops, and raise animals for food. We also use natural resources as fuel and a way to make electrical energy, or power. Natural resources that are used to make energy are called energy resources.

Petroleum Formation

As ocean plants and animals died, their remains were sometimes buried before they completely rotted away.

Nonrenewable Resources

Some natural resources are not easy to get back after they are gone. These resources are called **nonrenewable resources**. After a nonrenewable resource is used up, it takes millions of years to make more of it.

Nonrenewable resources include oil, natural gas, and coal. These resources are called **fossil fuels**. They are called fossil fuels because they come from the remains, or parts, of plants and animals that died long ago.

How did plants and animals change into oil? After they died, their remains sank to the ocean floor. Over time, sediments built up on top of the remains and pressed down on them. This pressure, along with heat from inside Earth, changed the remains into oil.

Over millions of years, heat and pressure turned these remains into oil.

The oil collected in cracks in rocks or in spaces between bits of sediment. Today, oil pumps take the oil from these spaces.

Renewable Resources

Not all natural resources are nonrenewable. Resources that are easy to make more of or that can be used over and over again are called **renewable resources**. Farm crops and animals are two renewable resources. So are oxygen and fresh water. Trees are renewable resources because new ones can always be grown.

Renewable resources that are used to make energy are called alternative energy sources. They can be used instead of fossil fuels. Some alternative energy sources are the Sun, wind, and water.

Solar Energy from the Sun is called solar energy. Two machines that can collect sunlight and change it into energy are solar panels and solar cells. Solar panels change sunlight into heat energy. Solar cells change sunlight into electricity.

Trees are an important natural resource. People use trees to make paper products and for lumber.

Cars powered by solar energy must carry a lot of solar cells.

In windy places, wind turbines can make a lot of energy.

Hydroelectric power is made by using the power of moving water to turn turbines. The energy from the spinning turbines is changed to electricity.

Wind Windmills have been used for hundreds of years to move water and to grind grain. Today, wind farms use rows of wind turbines to power machines that make electricity.

Wind turbines are like old-fashioned windmills. They have blades that turn as the wind blows. The energy from the moving blades is changed into electricity.

Water Moving water can be used to make electricity. Electrical power that is made from moving water is called hydroelectric power. Hydroelectric power is made by holding water behind a dam and slowly letting it out. The water turns turbines and the energy is changed to electricity.

Conservation

The wise, careful use of resources is called **conservation**. Conserving nonrenewable resources is very important because they cannot be replaced. By not wasting fossil fuels, you can save them for the future.

Another reason to conserve fossil fuels is to cut down on pollution. Pollution is anything that dirties our air, soil, and water. Smoke from burning fossil fuels can mix with water to form smog. Smog is not healthy to breathe.

Burning fuels adds a gas called carbon dioxide to the air. Earth may be slowly warming up from too much carbon dioxide in the air. This is called global warming. People are studying global warming to try to keep if from becoming a big problem.

Factories such as this one make many kinds of pollution.

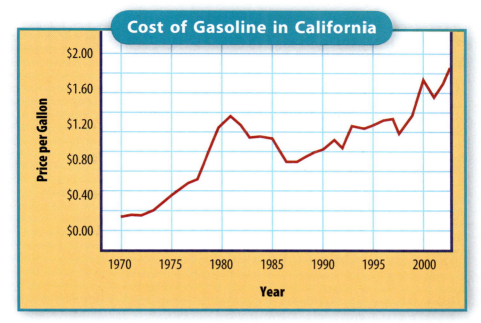

Cost of Gasoline in California

Price per Gallon

$2.00
$1.60
$1.20
$0.80
$0.40
$0.00

1970   1975   1980   1985   1990   1995   2000

Year

Most cars run on gasoline, a fossil fuel. As gasoline supplies are used up, the cost is likely to rise even higher.

Other waste gases from fossil fuels mix with water in the air to form acid rain, another kind of pollution. Acid rain can kill trees and fish, and harm buildings.

In many places, water is the most important natural resource to conserve. People need clean, fresh water for drinking, bathing, and growing crops. The world's need for water grows every year.

You and your family can help to conserve Earth's important resources by doing some simple things. Take trains and buses instead of a car. Or ride with other people. Turn off electric lights and appliances when not in use. Fix leaky faucets so they do not drip.

PROBLEM AND SOLUTION

How can people reduce their use of fossil fuels?

How Do People Use Soil?

One of the reasons soil is important is that crops and other plants grow in it. People must protect soil because rich, healthy soil takes a long time to form.

What Is Soil?

Soil is made up of minerals and small rocks, water, gases, and humus, or the remains of living things. A mineral is something found in Earth that is not living. Rocks and metals are minerals.

Not all soils are alike. Different places in the world have different kinds of soil. For example, the soil in a desert is very different from the soil in a forest.

The kind of soil a place has depends on several things. These include the usual weather in the place and the living matter in the place. The size of the particles, or bits, in the soil may describe the soil's texture, or how it feels.

SANDY SOIL In sandy soil, particles are medium-sized and very hard.

CLAY SOIL Clay soil is made up of very small, tightly packed mineral particles.

ROCKY SOIL Rocky soil, or gravel, includes fairly large pieces of rock.

How Soil Is Formed

Soil takes thousands of years to form. Soil begins with weathering. Weathering is the breaking down of rock into smaller pieces of rocks and minerals.

Deep under the soil is rock that has not been weathered. This rock is called bedrock. As the top part of the bedrock weathers, it breaks into smaller pieces. These pieces become part of the soil. Soil that forms from the bedrock under it is called **residual soil**.

Sometimes wind and water carry soil to another place. This soil, called **transported soil**, has minerals that are different from those in the bedrock below.

As soil forms, plants begin to grow. After plants and animals die, their remains decay, or rot away, to form humus. Humus has a lot of nutrients, or things that help living things grow.

Earthworms and other living things break down the remains of plants and animals. The remains make the soil rich.

Profile of Mature Soil

Over time, as soil forms, layers can be seen. These layers are called soil horizons. A mature, or fully formed, soil has four horizons. Young or immature soil has fewer horizons.

All of the soil horizons together are called a <mark>soil profile</mark>. In a mature soil profile, from the top down, the horizons are called topsoil, subsoil, parent material, and bedrock. The layers are also given letter names, as shown in the diagram.

Horizon A is the <mark>topsoil</mark>. Topsoil has humus, minerals, and rock pieces in it, as well as insects and earthworms. This part of the soil is the richest and is important for growing plants. Most plant seeds start to grow in topsoil.

HORIZON A
Topsoil

HORIZON B
Subsoil

HORIZON C
Parent Material

HORIZON D
Bedrock

Mature soil has four layers, or horizons.

Horizon B is the <mark>subsoil</mark>. Subsoil generally has very little humus. But water washes down some nutrients and remains from the topsoil. Some plant roots may reach down into the subsoil. Some earthworms and other living things may be found here.

The next layer, horizon C, is made up of chunks of partly weathered bedrock. This rock sometimes is called the parent material because the soil comes from it.

Below the parent material is the bedrock, or horizon D. The upper layers of soil rest on this thick layer of rock.

Plant roots, bits of dead plants, and remains of other living things make soil rich and healthy.

HORIZON A
Topsoil

HORIZON B
Subsoil

HORIZON C
Parent Material

HORIZON D
Bedrock

Protecting Topsoil

As you have learned, topsoil is the layer of soil that has the most nutrients. Plants use these nutrients almost the same way your body uses vitamins. The nutrients are not food for plants. But they are needed for healthy growth.

The nutrients are passed on to animals that eat the plants, and to animals that eat the plant-eaters. Material from these plants and animals then returns the nutrients to the soil. This cycle is important to all living things.

Farmers must work to keep nutrients in the soil. Growing crops take nutrients out of the soil. When the crops are picked, the nutrients are removed with them.

Growing crops need healthy topsoil with a lot of nutrients.

Crop Rotation Plan

	Field 1	Field 3	Field 5
Year 1	Wheat	Wheat	Wheat
Year 2	Canola	Canola	Corn
Year 3	Barley	Corn	Canola
Year 4	Flax	Sunflower	Flax
Year 5	Soybean	Barley	Alfalfa

This table shows some crop rotation plans for farms in northeast North Dakota.

How do farmers solve this problem? One way is by putting fertilizer in the soil. Fertilizer is powder or liquid that has nutrients in it. It can be added to soil to make the soil richer for crops. The problem with fertilizer is that some of it washes away when it rains.

Another way of returning nutrients to the soil is by crop rotation. Crop rotation is planting different crops during different growing seasons. Each kind of plant uses different kinds of nutrients.

If the same crop is grown in the same field for many years, the same nutrients are taken out of the soil. With crop rotation, the nutrients are put back into the soil naturally.

Conserving Topsoil

Farmers have found ways to keep soil from losing nutrients. However, topsoil also needs to be protected from wind, water, and other things that cause erosion.

What can happen if there is too much soil erosion? People learned the hard answer in the 1930s. Until then, many farmers in the Great Plains did not take care of the soil. As a result, crops sometimes were poor and there were no plants to hold down the topsoil. Things got worse during a long drought, or time without rain. The topsoil dried out and blew away. The places where this happened became known as the Dust Bowl.

In the Dust Bowl, huge dust storms swept across the fields. Winds carried soil far from the farmlands. Without topsoil, farmers could not grow crops for many years.

Today farmers follow much smarter soil conservation plans. One way farmers stop wind erosion of the topsoil is by planting windbreaks. A windbreak is a line of trees along the edge of a field. The trees help block the wind and stop or slow soil erosion.

Water is another cause of soil erosion. When water moves down the slopes of a plowed field, it picks up soil and carries it away. To slow this kind of erosion, farmers plow their fields in a special way. They follow the hills and curves in the land instead of plowing straight lines. This kind of plowing is called contour plowing. The winding rows slow water down as it runs down the slope.

Another way to stop soil erosion is to plant cover crops, such as clover or alfalfa. The roots of these plants hold soil in place and stop it from being carried away.

DRAW CONCLUSIONS

How do plants help protect soil?

3 How Can People Use Resources Wisely?

By using things over and over, by recycling, and by using smaller amounts of resources, people can help make sure that important resources will be there for people to use in years to come.

Using Resources Wisely

Think about some of the things you used today—a plastic water bottle, an aluminum can, a paper towel. These are very useful things, and all of them come from natural resources. Plastic is made from oil. Aluminum comes from a mineral that is mined. Paper is made from trees.

This can is made of aluminum. The three arrows mean that the can should be recycled. Then the aluminum can be used again.

When you were done with the bottle, can, and towel, what did you do with them? Did you throw them away? If so, the resources used to make these things were lost. But it doesn't have to be this way.

Recycling means taking a resource from one item and using that resource to make another item. For example, aluminum cans can be recycled to make new aluminum cans. Plastic bottles can be recycled to make cloth and other things. Recycling saves energy and conserves resources.

Look at the chart. Think about the trash that you throw out. Could you recycle some of it?

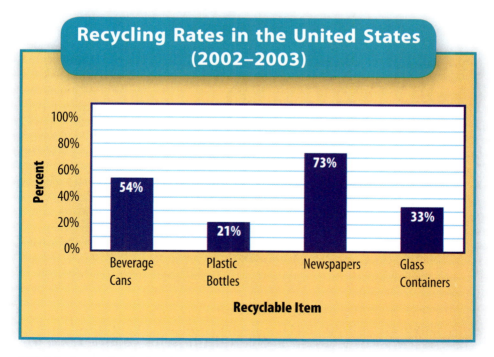

Recycling Rates in the United States (2002–2003)

Which item had the highest recycling rate in 2002–2003?

The Three Rs of Conservation

There are three main ways to conserve resources: reduce, reuse, and recycle. People call these the three Rs of conservation. You have already learned how recycling helps conserve resources.

Reducing just means that you use less material. When you use one paper towel to wipe up a spill instead of two, you reduce your use of paper. If you choose not to use a straw in your drink, you reduce the amount of plastic you use. Every time you walk or ride a bike instead of riding in a car, you reduce the amount of fossil fuels that you use.

This man is putting insulation in the wall of a house. Insulation helps keep a house cool in the summer and warm in the winter. In this way, it helps reduce the amount of energy used in buildings.

Reusing is another way to conserve resources. One way to reuse might be by washing an empty plastic pickle jar and keeping it on your desk as a pencil holder. This keeps the jar from ending up in the garbage. It also saves the material that would have been used to make a pencil holder that you might have bought at a store.

In general, reducing and reusing work better than recycling. Both save more resources and energy than recycling does. But recycling resources is still much better than wasting them.

Using things over and over again is part of using resources wisely. These containers and cloth diapers are just a few of the things that can be reused.

Where the Resources Are

Many resources are found only in certain parts of the world. In the past, people often lived in places where important resources were found. The natural resources that were in a place shaped the lives of the people. But today's transportation and technology make it much easier for people to use resources from all over the world.

People now often move resources from one place to another. A resource such as silver may be shipped from the place it is mined to another place where it will be turned into a form that people can use. Pure silver is then shipped all over the world to people who make jewelry and other useful things from silver.

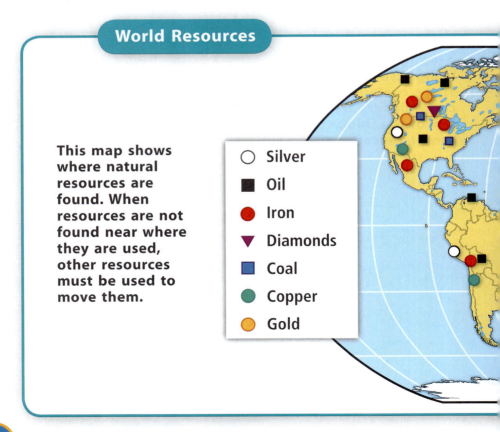

World Resources

This map shows where natural resources are found. When resources are not found near where they are used, other resources must be used to move them.

○ Silver
■ Oil
● Iron
▼ Diamonds
■ Coal
● Copper
● Gold

Oil is one resource that is used everywhere. But it is found in large amounts in only a few places. Every day, ships carry millions of gallons of oil across the oceans.

These ships sometimes have accidents, and the oil spills into the water. Oil spills can be deadly to fish, whales, seals, and other ocean life. Later, the oil can wash up on land and damage the shore and the animals and plants that live there.

Shipping resources around the world brings many benefits. But it can also cost a lot and harm the environment. When people conserve natural resources through the three Rs of conservation, fewer resources need to be shipped around the world.

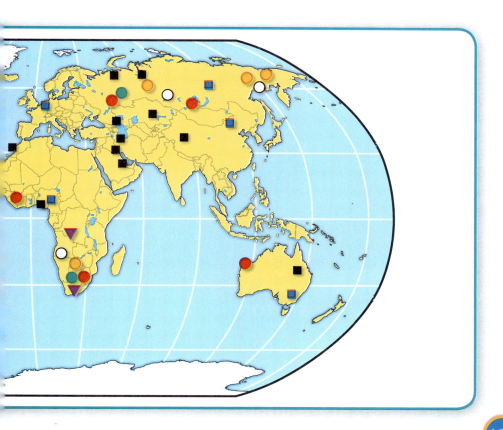

Landfills

Most trash that we throw away ends up in a landfill. A landfill is a place where trash is dumped and then sealed in with plastic or clay. This is good because it keeps the wastes from getting into the soil and water. On the other hand, it also slows down the rate at which the trash breaks down.

Garbage such as paper and leather break down fairly quickly when they are out in the open air. But when they are sealed in a landfill they may take years to break down. Other kinds of garbage may take hundreds of years to break down.

Landfills also take up a lot of space. When a landfill becomes full, a new one must be built.

When we reduce, reuse, and recycle, less garbage goes into landfills. Resources and land are conserved.

Landfills take up important land resources. When we reduce, reuse, and recycle, less trash needs to be sent to landfills.

PROBLEM AND SOLUTION

How does recycling help to conserve natural resources?

Glossary

conservation (kahn sur VAY shuhn), efficient use of resources

fossil fuel (FAHS uhl fyool),
    nonrenewable resource formed
    from ancient plants and animals

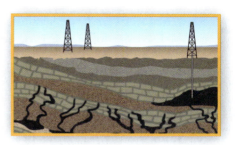

natural resource (NACH uhr uhl REE sawrs), resource found in nature,
    such as air, water, minerals, and soil

nonrenewable resource (nahn rih NOO uh buhl REE sawrs),
    resource, such as a fossil fuel, that is difficult to replace

recycling (ree SY klihng), process of recovering a resource from
    one item and using it to make another item

renewable resource (rih NOO uh buhl REE sawrs), resource,
    such as wind, that is easily replaced or renewed

Glossary

residual soil (rih ZIHJ oo uhl soyl), soil formed directly from the bedrock below it

soil (soyl), natural resource made up of small rocks, minerals, water, gases, and organic matter

soil profile (soyl PROH fyl), all of the soil horizons, or layers, in a soil sample

subsoil (SUHB soyl), layer of soil beneath the topsoil

topsoil (TAHP soyl), uppermost layer of soil

transported soil (trans PAWRT ihd soyl), soil that has been carried from one place to another by erosion

Responding

Think About What You Have Read

Vocabulary

❶ The practice of using all resources wisely is called
_____.

A) nonrenewable resource

B) natural resource

C) conservation

Comprehension

❷ Why is solar energy called a renewable resource?

❸ What layers make up a mature soil profile?

❹ What are three practices that help conserve natural resources?

Critical Thinking

❺ How would you respond to people who say it is not necessary to conserve fossil fuels, because the supply of fossil fuels will not run out during their lifetime?

Weather and Climate

Contents

1 What Factors Affect Climate?

Climate is the weather an area has over many years. The climate is affected by Earth's shape, the way Earth is tilted, and Earth's land and water.

Uneven Heating

Some places on Earth are warmer than others. That is because the Sun does not heat all places evenly.

The Sun's rays hit different parts of Earth at different angles. The Sun's rays hit places near the equator at a 90 degree angle. These places are warm all year long. In other places, such as the poles, the sun's rays hit at less than a 90 degree angle. These places are usually cooler.

Earth is not heated evenly. Some places are warmer than others.

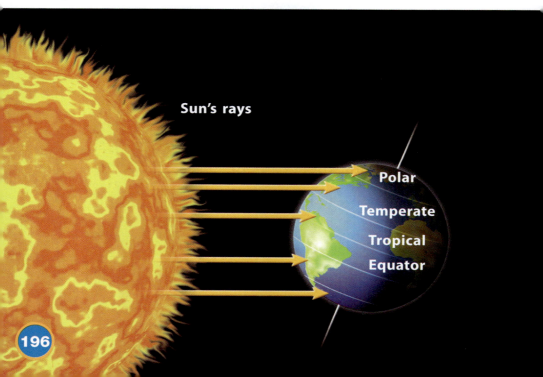

Sun's rays

Polar
Temperate
Tropical
Equator

Tropical: warm, rainy

Temperate: warm summer, cool winter

Polar: cold, snowy

Major Climate Zones

Climate is the normal pattern of weather in an area over many years. There are three major climate zones. Each one has different temperatures and different amounts of precipitation. Precipitation is any kind of water that falls from clouds, such as rain.

Tropical climates are found near the equator. They are very warm. It usually rains often in these climates. However some tropical areas get very little rain.

Temperate climates are found north or south of tropical climates. Some temperate climates have mild summers and winters. Others have warm summers with rain and cold winters with snow.

Polar climates are found near the North and South Poles. They are always cold and snowy.

Land and Sea Breezes

Shorelines are often windy places. These winds occur because the land and sea are not heated evenly. The unequal heating causes sea breezes and land breezes.

Sea breezes occur during the day. The land heats up faster than the water. The warm air over the land rises. Then cool air over the water moves in to take its place. Sea breezes blow from sea to land.

Land breezes occur at night. The land cools faster than the water, so the air over the water is warmer. The cool air over the land then moves toward the sea. Land breezes blow from land to sea.

Mountain Effect Precipitation

2 **Condensation: The water vapor cools and forms clouds.**

1 **Evaporation: Liquid water becomes water vapor, a gas.**

Mountain Effect

Some places near oceans have very rainy climates. Mountains often cause this.

First, water evaporates from the ocean and becomes water vapor in the air. The warm, moist air rises and moves toward the land. When the air meets the mountain, it is forced up into colder air. Cold air can hold less water vapor than warm air. The cold air makes the water vapor condense and form clouds.

Next, the clouds drop rain on the windward side of the mountain. That is the side where wind hits the mountain. Then the clouds pass to the other side, the leeward side, of the mountain. The clouds do not have much water vapor left in them, so very little rain falls on this side.

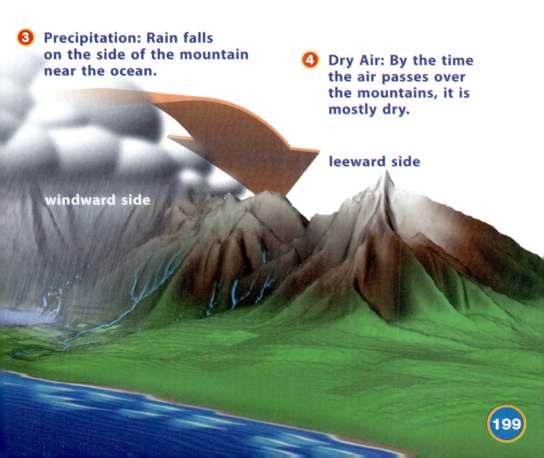

3 **Precipitation: Rain falls on the side of the mountain near the ocean.**

4 **Dry Air: By the time the air passes over the mountains, it is mostly dry.**

leeward side

windward side

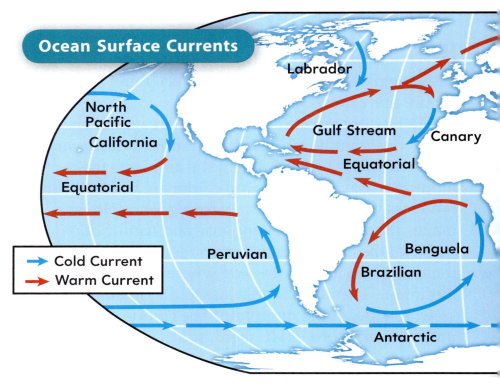

Ocean Surface Currents

Labrador

North Pacific

California

Gulf Stream

Canary

Equatorial

Equatorial

Equatorial

Peruvian

Benguela

Brazilian

Cold Current
Warm Current

Antarctic

The arrows on the map show ocean currents. The currents move water and energy from place to place.

Oceans and Climate

Most of the Earth's surface is covered by ocean water. Ocean waters take in huge amounts of energy from the Sun.

Places near the equator take in more energy from the Sun than do places near the poles. So ocean waters are warmest near the equator. They are coldest near the poles.

Air just above the warm ocean gets warmed by the water below. This warm air rises. Then cooler air moves in to take its place. This movement of air creates winds. Winds blowing across the ocean create moving streams of water called **ocean currents**.

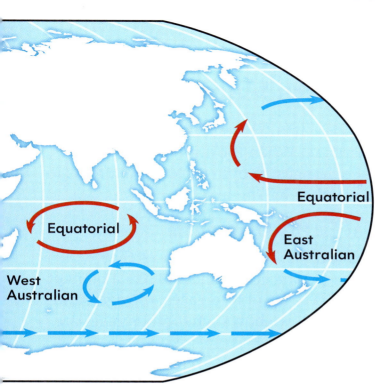

The map shows currents on the surface of the ocean. Some of the currents are warm. Others are cold. Warm currents move warm ocean water toward the poles. Cold currents move cold ocean water toward the equator. These currents make climates warmer or cooler.

Ocean currents can change from time to time. Sometimes warm ocean currents in the Pacific Ocean change their direction. This change is called El Niño. El Niño events occur every five to seven years. These events change the climate for a while in some places.

CAUSE AND EFFECT

How does uneven heating by the Sun affect climate on Earth?

2 How Are Weather Forecasts Made?

Gases surround the Earth. This blanket of gases is called the atmosphere. When the atmosphere changes, then the weather changes. People use different tools to learn what the weather will be like.

Composition of Earth's Atmosphere

Earth's **atmosphere** is a mixture of gases that surrounds the planet. The atmosphere is like a blanket of air. It is mostly made up of two gases, nitrogen and oxygen. The graph below shows what other gases are in the air.

Carbon dioxide is another gas in the atmosphere. The amount of carbon dioxide in the atmosphere can change. When more fossil fuels are burned on Earth, the amount of carbon dioxide goes up.

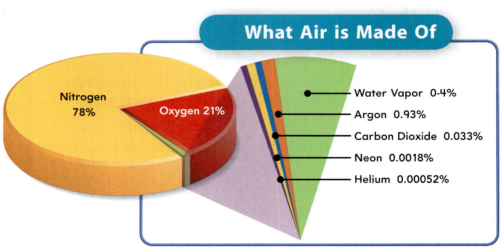

What Air is Made Of

Nitrogen 78%

Oxygen 21%

Water Vapor 0-4%

Argon 0.93%

Carbon Dioxide 0.033%

Neon 0.0018%

Helium 0.00052%

Air is mostly nitrogen and oxygen.

Structure of the Atmosphere

Earth's atmosphere has four layers. Each layer has a different temperature. The farther a layer is from Earth, the colder it is. These layers also cause air pressure, which affects Earth's weather.

The **troposphere** is the layer closest to Earth. This is where almost all weather takes place. It is the thinnest layer, but has most of the gases that make up the atmosphere in it. The next layer up is the **stratosphere**. It helps protect living things on Earth from the Sun's radiation. The third layer, the **mesosphere**, is the coldest part of the atmosphere. The fourth layer is the **thermosphere**. It is the first part of the atmosphere that sunlight hits.

Thermosphere

Mesosphere

Stratosphere

Troposphere

Air Masses

An **air mass** is a body of air that has about the same temperature and moisture throughout. The map shows different kinds of air masses in North America.

Some air masses are warm while others are cold. Air masses also have different amounts of moisture. Some are dry while others are moist. The amount of moisture depends on where the air mass is formed.

Continental air masses form over land and are dry. They usually bring fair weather. Maritime air masses form over water and are moist. They often bring fog and rain to coastal areas. They also bring moisture to the middle of the country.

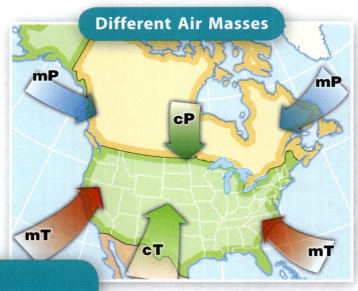

Different Air Masses

Key

mP maritime polar

cP continental polar

mT maritime tropical

cT continental tropical

Different air masses bring in warm, cold, moist, or dry air.

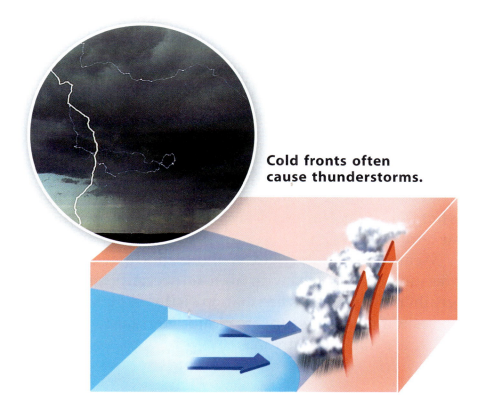

Cold fronts often cause thunderstorms.

Fronts

When two air masses meet, a front forms. A weather <mark>front</mark> is the boundary between two air masses that have different properties. For example, one air mass may be cool and the other may be warm. Most fronts change the weather.

Warm fronts often bring clouds and light rain. A warm front is shown with a red line on a weather map. Cold fronts often bring heavy rain or thunderstorms. A cold front is shown with a blue line on a weather map. Sometimes two air masses meet but neither one moves forward. This is called a stationary front.

Observing Weather

Meteorologists are scientists who study weather. They make observations. They study data, too. Then they record their findings on a weather map. When they study the map, they can tell what the future weather will be like.

Weather maps have symbols. These symbols show what the weather is like in different places. A key tells what the symbols mean. Maps also use colors to show air temperatures.

Weather maps show areas of high and low air pressure. Most places with high air pressure have clear weather. These places are marked with an H. Most places with low pressure are cloudy and rainy. These places are marked with an L.

Maps can be used to predict the weather.

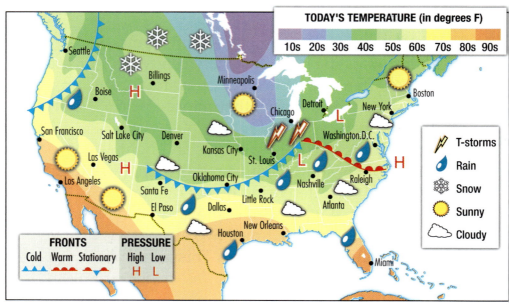

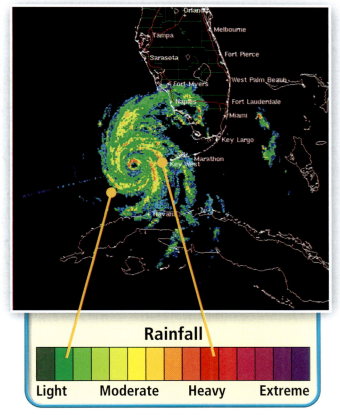

Rainfall

Light   Moderate   Heavy   Extreme

Green shows light rain. Red shows heavy rain.

Radar

Radar can be used to observe the weather. It can help tell what the weather will be like.

Radar shows where rain or snow is falling. It makes a picture of the storm. The radar picture above shows Hurricane Charley that hit Florida in 2004. The picture has different colors. The colors show how much rain fell in different places.

Radar can show the size of a storm. It can also show how fast the storm is moving, and where it is headed. Meteorologists can use this information to warn people about dangerous storms.

Other Weather Instruments

Satellites are also used to learn about weather. These machines orbit high above Earth. They gather information about the atmosphere and send it back to meteorologists. Satellites can also be used to study clouds and storms.

Other tools are used to measure weather. Thermometers measure temperature. Rain gauges measure the amount of rain or snow.

Anemometers measure wind speed.

Barometers measure air pressure.

Weather vanes show which way the wind is blowing.

DRAW CONCLUSIONS

How do air masses affect weather?

Glossary

air mass (air mas), huge volume of air responsible for types of weather

atmosphere (AT muh sfihr), mixture of gases that surrounds Earth

climate (KLY miht), normal pattern of weather that occurs in an area over a long period of time

El Niño (ehl NEE nyo), periodic change in the direction of warm ocean currents across the Pacific Ocean

front (fruhnt), narrow region between two air masses that have different properties

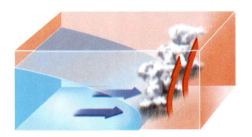

Glossary

mesosphere (mehz oh sfeer), layer of the atmosphere above the stratosphere and below the thermosphere

ocean current (OH shuhn KUR uhnt), moving stream of water created by winds pushing against the ocean's surface

stratosphere (STRA tuh sfeer), layer of the atmosphere above the troposphere and below the mesosphere

thermosphere (THUHR muh sfeer), the outermost layer of the atmosphere, above the mesosphere

troposphere (TROH puh sfihr), layer of Earth's atmosphere closest to Earth's surface and containing about three-quarters of the atmosphere's gases

Responding

Think About What You Have Read

Vocabulary

❶ Earth's _____ is a mixture of gases that surround the planet.

A) atmosphere

B) climate

C) front

D) ocean currents

Comprehension

❷ What are some factors that affect climate?

❸ What are the four main layers of Earth's atmosphere?

❹ Why are weather satellites an important tool for meteorologists?

Critical Thinking

❺ How might radar images help to reduce damage from an approaching storm?

Earth and Its Moon

Contents

1

What Causes Earth's Seasons?

Earth rotates on its axis, causing day and night. Earth revolves around the Sun, causing the seasons.

Earth's Tilted Axis

Earth always rotates, or spins around. It rotates around an imaginary line called an **axis**. The axis is like a line that goes from the North Pole through the center of Earth to the South Pole. This line is not straight up and down. It is tilted at an angle of 23 ½ degrees.

It takes 23 hours and 56 minutes for Earth to rotate once around. This time period is called a day. As Earth rotates, different parts face the Sun. The side of Earth facing the Sun has daytime. The side facing away from the Sun has nighttime.

Sun and Earth in June

Summer in the Northern Hemisphere

Winter in the Southern Hemisphere

Earth's tilt causes the seasons.

Earth also moves around the Sun. One full trip around the Sun is called a **revolution**. It takes one year, or 365 ¼ days, to make one revolution.

Earth's axis is tilted. Some parts of Earth tilt toward the Sun during a revolution. Other parts tilt away from the Sun. The tilt causes the seasons.

It is summer when part of Earth tilts toward the Sun. It is winter when part of Earth tilts away from the Sun.

Study the photographs on pages 214 and 215. They show that when it is summer in the Northern Hemisphere, it is winter in the Southern Hemisphere.

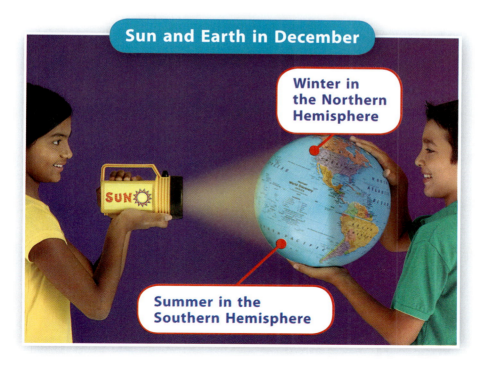

Sun and Earth in December

Winter in the Northern Hemisphere

SUN

Summer in the Southern Hemisphere

Solstices and Equinoxes

In the Northern Hemisphere, the longest day of the year is June 21 or 22. On this day, the North Pole points *toward* the Sun. This is the **summer solstice** and marks the start of summer.

The shortest day of the year is the **winter solstice** on December 21 or 22. This marks the start of winter. On this day, the North Pole points directly *away* from the Sun.

There are two equinoxes each year. These are days when there is the same amount of sunlight and darkness everywhere on Earth. The **vernal equinox** is on March 21 or 22 and marks the start of spring. The **autumnal equinox** is on September 22 or 23 and marks the start of fall.

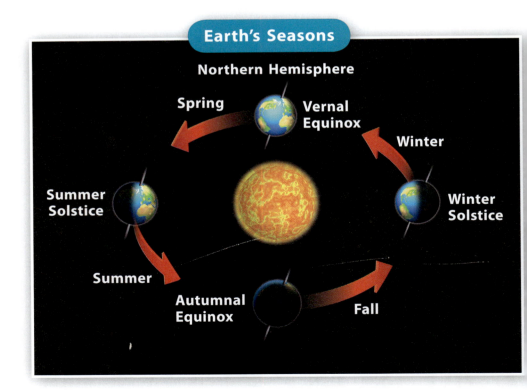

Earth's Seasons

Northern Hemisphere

Spring

Vernal Equinox

Winter

Summer Solstice

Winter Solstice

Summer

Autumnal Equinox

Fall

Seasons

All places on Earth have four seasons: spring, summer, fall, and winter. Not all places on Earth feel the seasons in the same way.

Near the poles, the Sun's rays hit at sharp angles. These places, such as McMurdo on the South Pole, have cold weather all year long. Near the equator, the Sun's rays hit more directly. These places, such as Panama City, have mostly warm weather.

Some places feel the seasons more strongly. Chicago, Illinois and Santiago, Chile are about halfway between the equator and a pole. Their temperatures go up and down a lot. This shows that a place's position on Earth has a big effect on the place's weather and seasons.

Chicago
Panama City
Santiago
McMurdo

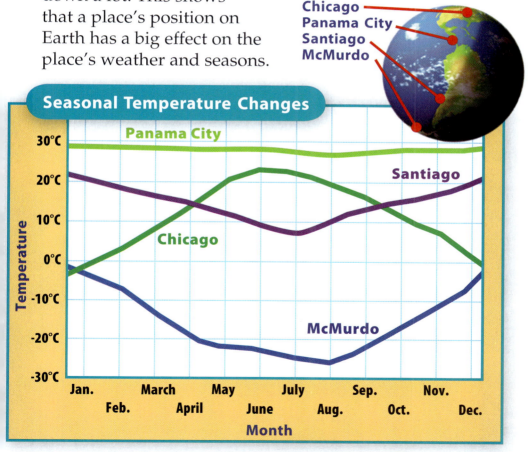

Seasonal Temperature Changes

An area's position on Earth affects the weather there.

Ideas About the Sun

Hundreds of years ago, people did not know much about the Sun. They had false ideas about it. That means that the thoughts they had about the Sun were actually wrong. For example, people used to think that Earth was the center of the universe. They thought the Sun revolved around Earth.

Galileo was an astronomer. An astronomer is a person who studies the skies. In the 1600s he wrote a book that said that Earth revolved around the Sun. He also explained why this happened. He was arrested for telling others about his idea.

Today, we know that Galileo was correct. Based on his work, scientists can tell where Earth, the Sun, and other objects will appear in the sky.

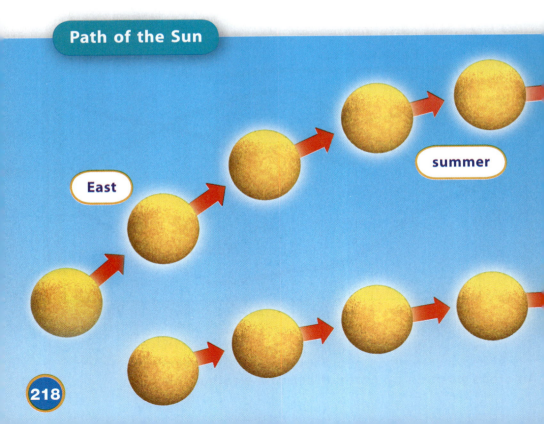

Path of the Sun

East

summer

People had other false ideas, too. They thought that the seasons came because of Earth's distance from the Sun. We now know that Earth is actually closer to the Sun in December than in June. We also know that the seasons are caused by Earth's tilted axis and revolutions around the Sun. Because of the tilt, the Sun rises higher in the sky. This makes summer days last longer.

Study the picture. It shows how the Sun seems to travel across the sky in the Northern Hemisphere. The Sun is higher in the summer, so the days are longer and warmer.

CAUSE AND EFFECT

Why do the Northern and Southern hemispheres have opposite seasons?

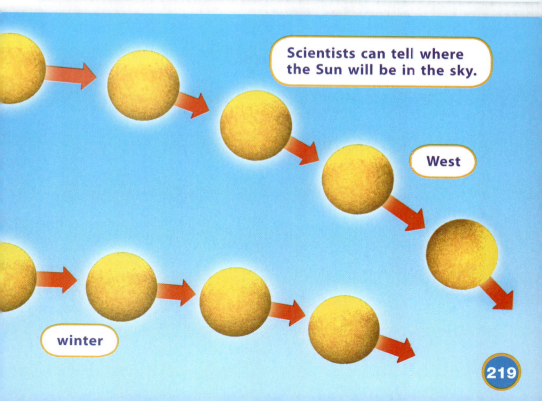

Scientists can tell where the Sun will be in the sky.

West

winter

2

Why Does the Moon Have Phases?

The Moon revolves around Earth, and they revolve around the Sun together. The same side of the Moon always faces Earth, but the Sun lights up different parts of the Moon at different times.

The Moon

A satellite is an object that revolves around Earth. The Moon is a satellite. It is Earth's only natural satellite.

The Moon is a sphere, or round like a ball. It is much smaller than Earth, and is 80 times lighter. Compared to Earth, the Moon does not have a very strong gravitational pull. Because of this, there is not much of an atmosphere around the Moon. Its gravity, though, is strong enough to affect Earth's tides.

The Moon revolves around Earth.

There are rocks on the surface of the Moon. They are about 4.6 billion years old.

Viewing the Moon

At night, the Moon seems to be the biggest and brightest object in the sky. It is really much smaller than the other objects, though. It just looks large because it is so close to Earth. The planet Venus is about the same size as Earth. It looks like a small dot in the sky. Because the Moon is closer to Earth, it looks much larger than Venus.

The Moon looks bright at night. However, it does not produce any light. It looks bright because the Sun is shining on it. That is why you can see the Moon from Earth.

Like Earth, the Moon rotates on an imaginary axis. One full rotation takes 27 ⅓ days. The Moon also revolves, but around Earth, not the Sun. It takes 27 ⅓ days for the Moon to revolve around Earth. As you can see, the Moon takes the same period of time to rotate and revolve. Because of this, the same side of the Moon always faces Earth.

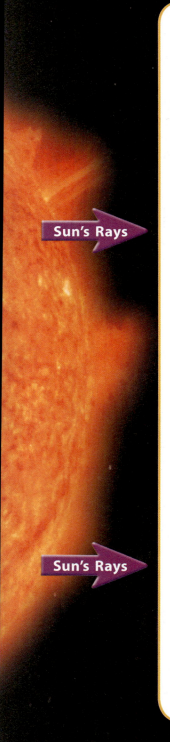

Sun's Rays

Sun's Rays

Phases of the Moon

The Sun is always shining on the Moon so one half of the Moon is always lit up. Because the Moon revolves around Earth, the entire lit up half is not visible. Only parts of the lighted half can be seen. The shapes created by the changing amounts of the visible lighted areas are called **Moon phases**. A complete cycle of the Moon phases takes about one month.

The first phase is the new Moon. In this phase, the Moon is between Earth and the Sun. The lit side of the Moon is facing away from Earth. So the Moon appears dark.

The Moon continues to revolve around Earth. Now more of the lit area can be seen. The next phase is called waxing crescent. The Moon appears to be waxing, or growing. Soon half of the lit area can be seen. Now the Moon is in its first quarter phase. More and more of the Moon is visible until the full Moon phase is reached. In this phase, the entire lit side can be seen.

The Moon then appears to be waning, or getting smaller. Less of the lit side can be seen. The phases at this point in the revolution are called waning gibbous, last quarter, and waning crescent.

Phases of the Moon

last quarter

waning gibbous

waning crescent

full moon

new moon

waxing gibbous

waxing crescent

first quarter

Eclipses

An eclipse is when one object passes into the shadow of another object. Sometimes Earth, the Sun, and the Moon are lined up in a straight line. This can form two kinds of eclipses.

A **solar eclipse** takes place when the Moon passes between the Sun and Earth. The Moon blocks the light from the Sun. This makes a shadow on Earth.

The shadow has two parts. One part is darker than the other. The darker part of the shadow is called the umbra. The parts of Earth in this area have a total solar eclipse. The lighter part of the shadow is the penumbra. The parts of Earth in this area have a partial solar eclipse.

Solar Eclipse

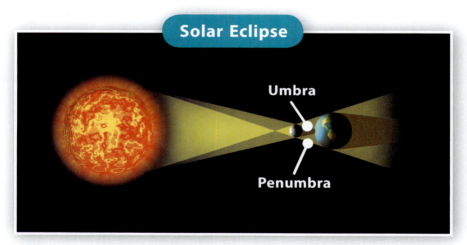

Umbra

Penumbra

The Moon goes between the Sun and Earth.

A total solar eclipse

A **lunar eclipse** takes place when Earth passes directly between the Sun and the Moon. The Moon then moves into Earth's shadow.

A total lunar eclipse takes place when the entire Moon passes into the umbra, or darker part, of Earth's shadow. The Moon can still be seen during this time, but it looks different. It has a reddish color. During a partial lunar eclipse, only part of the Moon passes into the umbra. The rest of the Moon is in the penumbra.

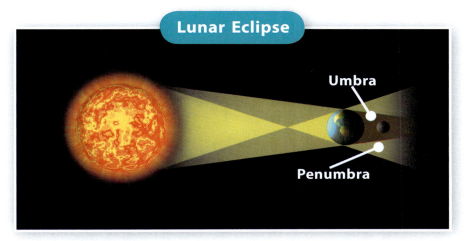

Lunar Eclipse

Umbra

Penumbra

Earth goes between the
Sun and the Moon.

A total lunar eclipse

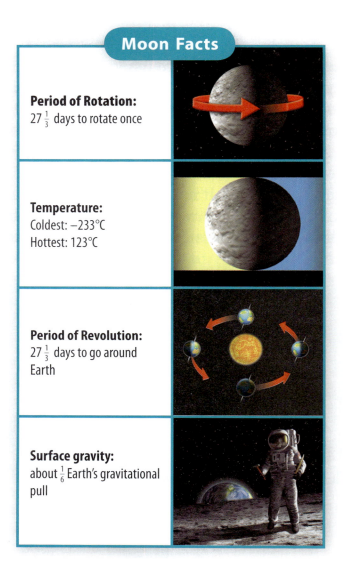

Moon Facts

Period of Rotation:
$27\frac{1}{3}$ days to rotate once

Temperature:
Coldest: $-233°C$
Hottest: $123°C$

Period of Revolution:
$27\frac{1}{3}$ days to go around Earth

Surface gravity:
about $\frac{1}{6}$ Earth's gravitational pull

SEQUENCE

Why does the Moon go through phases?

Glossary

autumnal equinox (aw TUHM nuhl EE kwuh nahks), September 22 or 23, when the number of hours of daylight and darkness are the same

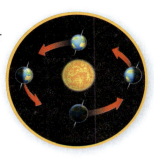

axis (AK sihs), imaginary line that goes through the center of Earth from the North Pole to the South Pole

lunar eclipse (LOO nuhr ih KLIHPS), when Earth passes directly between the Sun and the Moon, casting a shadow on the Moon

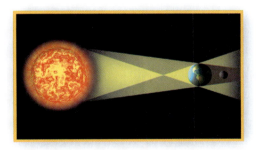

Moon phases (moon FAYZ ihz), shapes created by the changing amounts of the visible lighted areas of the Moon

revolution (rehv uh LOO shuhn), one full trip, or orbit, around the Sun

Glossary

solar eclipse (SOH luhr ih KLIHPS), when the Moon passes directly between the Sun and Earth, casting a shadow on Earth

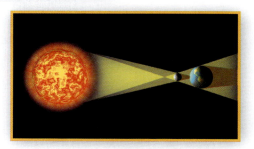

summer solstice (SUHM uhr SAHL stihs), June 21 or 22, the longest day of the year in the Northern Hemisphere

vernal equinox (VUR nuhl EE kwuh nahks), March 20 or 21, when the number of hours of daylight and darkness are the same

winter solstice (WIHN tuhr SAHL stihs), December 21 or 22, the shortest day of the year in the Northern Hemisphere

Responding

Think About What You Have Read

Vocabulary

1 What happens during a total solar eclipse?

A) The Moon blocks out all of the Sun.

B) The Sun blocks out all of the Moon.

C) The Moon blocks out part of the Sun.

D) The Sun blocks out part of the Moon.

Comprehension

2 Why is the same side of the Moon always visible from Earth?

3 What causes day and night? What causes seasons?

4 Why can you see the Moon from Earth?

Critical Thinking

5 Explain why the shortest day of the year in the Northern Hemisphere is on December 21 or 22. Where is this the longest day?

Exploring Space

Contents

1   What Orbits the Sun?

The Sun and the bodies that revolve, or travel, around it make up the solar system. The solar system is part of a much larger galaxy called the Milky Way.

The Sun and Its Neighbors

The **solar system** is made up of the Sun and all the bodies that revolve around it. The solar system has eight major planets and several dwarf planets. A **planet** is a large body that revolves around the Sun. Earth is a planet. The planets do not make their own light. They shine because the Sun's light shines on them.

The Sun is the largest part of the solar system. The other bodies in the solar system are held in their positions by the Sun's gravity. Many planets, like Earth, have one or more moons. The solar system also has asteroids, comets, and meteorites.

Neptune

Jupiter

Mars

Uranus

Pluto

Scientists think that the solar system formed about 4.6 billion years ago. First, there was a hot cloud of gases and dust. The cloud began to spin. Then gravity pulled the gases and dust toward the center of the cloud. The cloud became flat and hot. Great heat and pressure built up near the center. This caused nuclear reactions and these reactions formed the Sun.

Planets and moons formed in the cooler part of the cloud. Planets close to the Sun were made of rocky material. The ones farther away held more gases, so they were larger. Asteroids, comets, and meteorites also formed.

The Sun has strong gravity. The Sun's gravity keeps all of the planets and objects traveling around the Sun. The path that each object travels around the Sun is called its orbit.

The solar system includes the Sun, nine planets, and other smaller objects.

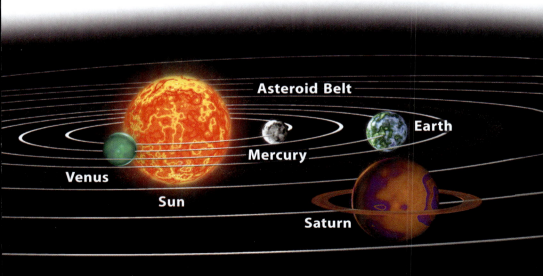

Moons

There are about 140 moons in the solar system. These moons are held in orbit by the gravitational pull of their planets. Not all moons are like Earth's Moon. Some moons have an atmosphere. Other moons seem to have water or ice beneath their surfaces. One moon has volcanoes.

Asteroids

An **asteroid** is a small, rocky object that orbits the Sun. There are millions of them in the solar system. Most of them orbit in a band called the asteroid belt. This is located between Mars and Jupiter.

Some asteroids may be hundreds of kilometers across. Others are small. They are only a few meters across. Asteroids come in different shapes. Some look like baked potatoes!

Io is a moon of Jupiter. Io has many volcanoes.

Asteroids are small and rocky. Many orbit the Sun between Mars and Jupiter.

Comets

A **comet** is a small, orbiting body made of dust, ice, and frozen gases. Comets orbit the Sun. The orbits of most comets are elliptical. This means that the comet passes close to the Sun, then swings far away from it.

Comets have a cold center. When a comet comes near the Sun, part of it starts to glow. This is called a coma. Energy from the Sun makes the coma grow, and a glowing tail forms. The tail can be millions of kilometers long.

Some comets make one complete trip around the Sun in fewer than 200 years. These are called short–period comets. Long–period comets travel much farther away from the Sun. They may take 30 million years to orbit the Sun!

Comet orbits are elliptical. The comet's tail always points away from the Sun.

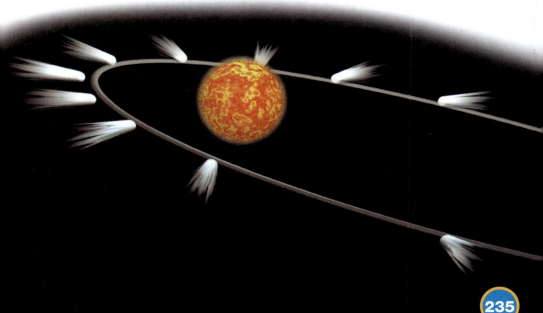

Meteors

Have you ever seen a "shooting star"? These streaks of light are not moving stars. They are meteors.

A **meteor** is a streak of light caused by a chunk of matter that enters Earth's atmosphere and is heated by friction with the air around it. One of these chunks of matter is called a **meteoroid**. The meteoroid burns as it falls. This forms streaks of light in the night sky. Some meteoriods are large, like asteroids. Most are much smaller. Many are smaller than a grain of sand.

Sometimes many meteors can be seen at the same time. This is called a meteor shower. In some meteor showers, 50 meteors can be seen each hour. Meteor showers can last a few hours. Some last for a few days.

This is a meteor shower. Several meteors are falling at once.

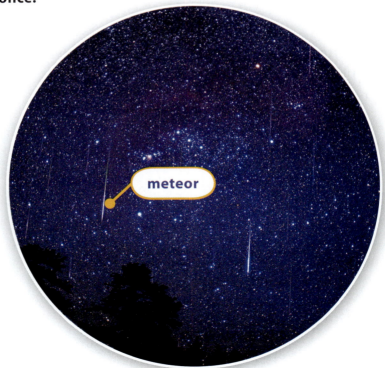

meteor

The Barringer Crater was formed when a large meteorite fell to Earth.

Sometimes a meteor stays together as it falls through Earth's atmosphere. When it hits the ground, it is called a <mark>meteorite</mark>. Most meteorites seem to come from the asteroid belt.

Large meteorites can hit Earth's surface. When they do, they form impact craters. These are like large, bowl-shaped holes on Earth. Look at the picture. It shows the Barringer Crater. This was formed in Arizona when a meteorite hit there thousands of years ago.

TEXT STRUCTURE

How is a meteorite different from a meteor?

2

What Are the Planets Like?

The solar system has eight major planets and several dwarf planets. The four major planets closest to the Sun are the inner planets. The other four are the outer planets.

The Inner Planets

Mercury, Venus, Earth, and Mars are the first four planets from the Sun. They are closer to the Sun than the other planets. So they are called the **inner planets**.

The inner planets have some things in common. They are all rocky. Also, they are all smaller than most of the other planets. Each of the inner planets, though, is different from Earth and from each other.

Mercury is the planet closest to the Sun. It has many craters.

Sun

Venus has a few craters. It has a thick atmosphere.

Mercury is the smallest inner planet. It is the one closest to the Sun. During the day, Mercury is very hot. At night, it is very cold.

Venus is the second planet from the Sun. It is below a thick layer of clouds. Its atmosphere is made mostly of poisonous gases.

Earth is the third planet from the Sun. It is the only planet known to have liquid water. Earth's atmosphere and oceans keep the temperature not too hot and not too cold. This allows life on Earth.

Mars is the fourth planet from the Sun. It is called the red planet. Mars is smaller than Earth. It has a flat, rocky surface, with deep canyons and a very large volcano.

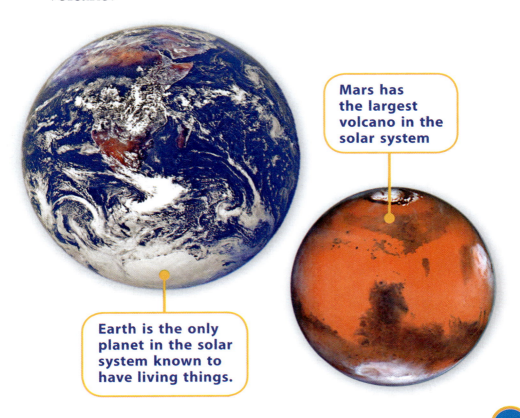

Mars has the largest volcano in the solar system

Earth is the only planet in the solar system known to have living things.

The Outer Planets

The **outer planets** are Jupiter, Saturn, Uranus, Neptune, and Pluto. These planets, except for Pluto, are larger than the inner planets. They are mostly made of gases.

Jupiter is the fifth planet from the Sun. It has strong winds that produce bands, or stripes. The planet also has a huge storm. The storm is called the Great Red Spot. Jupiter has many moons, and also some rings made up of particles from meteors.

Saturn is the sixth planet from the Sun. It is known for its rings. The rings are made mostly of ice. Saturn is a large planet. It can hold more than 95 Earths. But it is the least dense of any planet. If you could put Saturn on water, it would float!

Jupiter is the largest planet in the solar system.

Saturn's rings are made of many small particles.

Uranus is the seventh planet from the Sun. The axis of Uranus is tilted much more than the other planets. Because of this, Uranus seems to be "lying" on its side. Uranus has rock and ice in its middle. The rest of the planet is gases.

Neptune is the eighth planet from the Sun. It is the windiest planet. Winds there can reach 2,700 km/h (1,500 mph)! Neptune has at least 11 moons. It also has rings, but they look different than the rings of other planets.

Pluto is much smaller than the other outer planets. Pluto is called a dwarf planet. Sometimes its orbit brings it closer to the Sun than Neptune. Pluto is small, icy, and rocky. It is very cold.

Uranus has a green color.

Pluto has ice at its poles.

Neptune's largest moon is called Triton.

Exploring Space

Optical telescopes are used to explore the solar system and space. To use one of these, a person looks through lenses. This makes the object look larger and brighter. Many telescopes today also have cameras and computers. These are used to make pictures of the objects. They are also used to gather information about the objects.

Telescopes are affected by Earth's atmosphere. The atmosphere has clouds and gases. It is sometimes hard for the telescope to "see" through these things into space. Because of this, many telescopes are set up on mountains. Others are in orbit around Earth.

This Mars Rover gathers information about Mars.

This space probe takes pictures of Mars.

The space shuttle is a vehicle that takes equipment and people into space. As it orbits Earth, scientists do experiments. After a while, it returns to Earth.

A space station stays in space for a long time. Scientists and astronauts can live and sleep there. They do experiments there, too.

A space probe carries special equipment into space. Some probes are placed into Earth's upper atmosphere. Others go much farther into space. The Mars Rovers Spirit and Opportunity traveled to Mars. They studied rocks and dirt.

COMPARE AND CONTRAST

What are some ways that the inner planets are the same?

3

What Are Stars Like?

A star is made of gases. Stars change over time.
The Sun is a medium-sized star. It is about halfway
through its life cycle.

Earth's Star: the Sun

The sky is filled with stars. A <mark>star</mark> is a large sphere
of glowing gases. A star has nuclear reactions in its
center, or core. Because of this, energy gets released
into space. Stars in the sky seem to twinkle when the
energy moves through Earth's atmosphere.

The Sun is a yellow star made mostly of hydrogen
and helium. The surface of the Sun is about 5,500°C
(9,932°F). Many stars are hotter and larger than the
Sun. Many other stars are smaller and cooler. Some are
even larger and *cooler*!

**The Sun is much larger than Earth. It looks smaller because
it is so far away.**

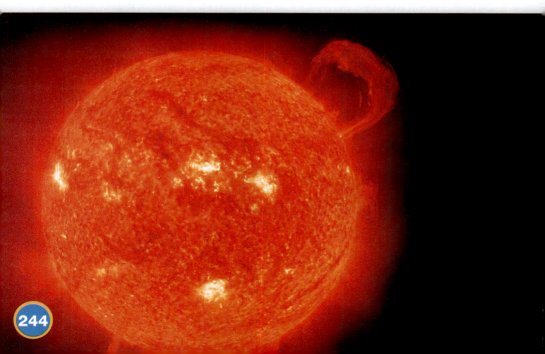

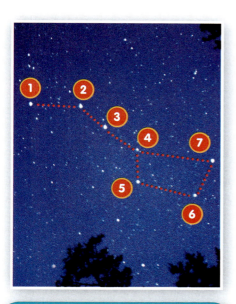

Stars in the Big Dipper

Star Name	Distance from Earth
1 Alkaid	108 Ly
2 Mizar	59 Ly
3 Alioth	62 Ly
4 Megrez	65 Ly
5 Phecda	75 Ly
6 Merak	62 Ly
7 Dubhe	75 Ly

Outside of the solar system, objects in space are far away from each other. Astronomers measure these distances using light-years. A **light-year**, or Ly, is the distance that light travels in one year. That is about 9.5 trillion km.

For hundreds of years, people have seen patterns in the stars. These patterns are called constellations. The Big Dipper is a pattern in a larger constellation. It is easy to see at night.

The chart on this page shows how many light-years away the stars of the Big Dipper are from Earth.

There are billions of stars. Most of them are very far from Earth. You can see them because they are so bright. The brightness of a star is called its **magnitude**. Most of the time, bigger stars have greater magnitudes than smaller stars. Stars that are closer to Earth look brighter.

A Star Is Born

Stars are not alive, but they go through changes like a life cycle. The path a star takes through its life cycle depends on its mass.

A star begins as a rotating cloud of dust and gas called a nebula. The cloud starts to rotate faster and forms a **protostar**, the first stage in the formation of a star. The protostar gets hotter and starts to glow. Then it becomes a star.

Next, it becomes a main sequence star. It will give off energy for millions of years. These stars are different colored. Blue or white ones are the hottest and brightest. Most medium-sized stars are yellow or orange. The coolest and least bright stars are red.

The Sun is a medium-sized star. It is about halfway through its life cycle.

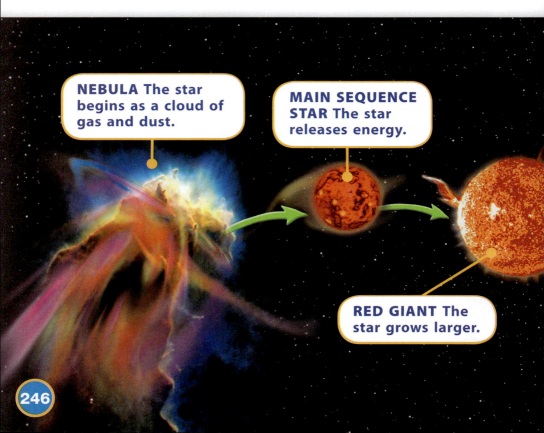

NEBULA The star begins as a cloud of gas and dust.

MAIN SEQUENCE STAR The star releases energy.

RED GIANT The star grows larger.

Next, the core, or inner part of the star, starts to get smaller. The outer part gets bigger. It is now called a red giant. From here, the star can follow one of two paths. The path it goes down is based on the star's mass.

Medium-sized red giants keep giving off energy. After all the "fuel" in the core is used up, it becomes a white dwarf. After that, it becomes a black dwarf.

Massive, or very large, red giants go down another path. These stars heat up and then explode. This explosion is called a supernova. After this, the star will sometimes become a neutron star. Other red giants become something called a black hole.

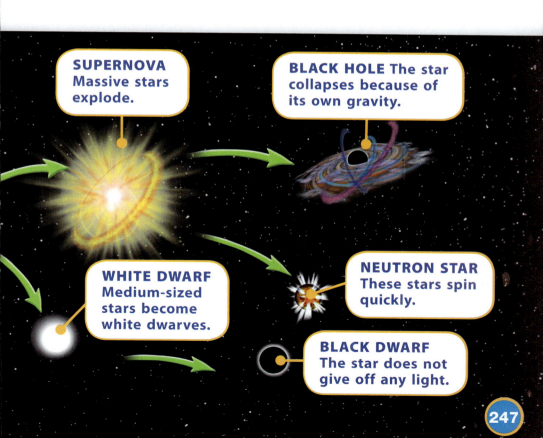

SUPERNOVA Massive stars explode.

BLACK HOLE The star collapses because of its own gravity.

WHITE DWARF Medium-sized stars become white dwarves.

NEUTRON STAR These stars spin quickly.

BLACK DWARF The star does not give off any light.

Galaxies

A **galaxy** is an enormous system of gases, dust, and stars, all held together by gravity. Small galaxies have hundreds of thousands of stars. Large ones have billions of stars. It is not known how many galaxies there are in the universe. Some scientists think that there are about 125 billion of them.

Most galaxies have two main parts. The bulge is the part of the galaxy where there are old stars, gases, and dust. The halo has old stars and dark matter. Dark matter is matter that cannot be seen or touched. Much of the universe is made of dark matter.

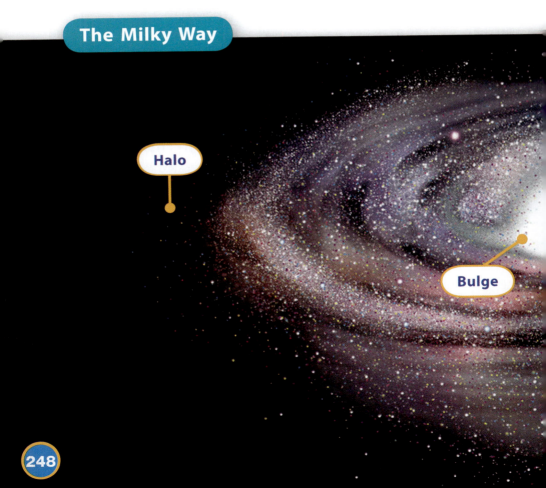

The Milky Way

Halo

Bulge

The Milky Way

Our solar system is part of the Milky Way galaxy. There are over 200 billion stars in this galaxy. The Sun is just one of them. If you could see the Milky Way galaxy from outer space, it would look like the picture on this page.

One part of the Milky Way galaxy is the disk. Most of the galaxy's stars, gas, and dust are found in the disk. The disk is a flattened area. It has young stars and dust. It is about 100,000 Ly across. Our solar system is located in the disk. It is about 28,000 Ly from the center of the galaxy. The Milky Way's halo is more than 130,000 Ly across.

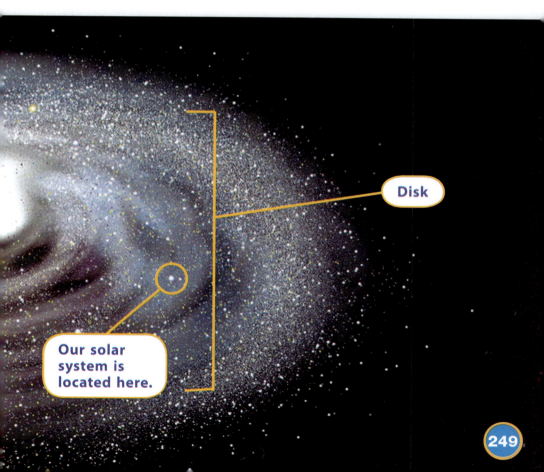

Disk

Our solar system is located here.

Types of Galaxies

The Milky Way galaxy is a spiral galaxy. This is one kind of galaxy. There are three types of galaxies: spiral, elliptical, and irregular.

All spiral galaxies have bulges, halos, and disks. In some spiral galaxies, the "arms" come out of the bulge. This is how the Milky Way galaxy is. Not all spiral galaxies are the same. In other ones, the arms do not come out of the bulge. They come out of an object that is shaped like a bar. This bar runs through the bulge.

Spiral Galaxy

A spiral galaxy has arms that come out of the bulge.

Elliptical galaxies are shaped like a flat ball. They do not have arms like spiral galaxies do. These galaxies are brightest at their centers. That is where the bulge is.

Irregular galaxies have stars, gases, and dust. They do not have a real shape, though. These galaxies have a lot of hydrogen gas. They also have many young, hot stars.

Galaxies are too far away to study with space vehicles. Scientists study galaxies with telescopes that are in space.

Elliptical Galaxy

An elliptical galaxy is shaped like a flattened ball.

Irregular Galaxy

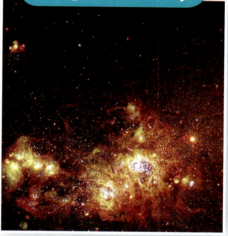

An irregular galaxy does not have a shape.

MAIN IDEA

Describe the three major types of galaxies.

Glossary

asteroid (AS tuh royd), small, rocky object that orbits the Sun

comet (KAHM iht), small orbiting body made of dust, ice, and frozen gases

galaxy (GAL uhk see), an enormous system of gases, dust, and stars held together by gravity

inner planets (IHN uhr PLAN ihtz), the four major planets of the solar system that are closest to the sun — Mercury, Venus, Earth, and Mars

light–year (LYT yihr), unit of measurement for distances outside the solar system and equal to about 9.5 trillion km

magnitude (MAG nih tood), brightness of a star as perceived from Earth

meteor (MEE tee uhr), chunk of matter that enters Earth's atmosphere and is heated by friction with the air

Glossary

meteorite (MEE tee uh ryt), a chunk of meteor matter that falls to the ground

meteoroid (MEE tee uh royd), a chunk of matter moving through space

outer planets (OW tuhr PLAN ihtz), the major planets of the solar system farthest from the Sun—Jupiter, Saturn, Uranus, and Neptune

planet (PLAN iht), a large body that revolves around the Sun

protostar (PROH tuh stahr), first stage in the formation of a star

solar system (SOH luhr SIHS tuhm), the Sun and all bodies that revolve around it

star (stahr), giant sphere of glowing gases

Think About What You Have Read

Vocabulary

❶ Small, rocky objects that orbit the Sun between Mars and Jupiter are called _____.

A) meteors

B) meteorites

C) comets

D) asteroids

Comprehension

❷ What different types of bodies make up the solar system?

❸ Compare and contrast the characteristics of Earth with those of its two nearest neighbors.

❹ What is a star?

Critical Thinking

❺ Why do you think the outer planets have so many moons?

Cells

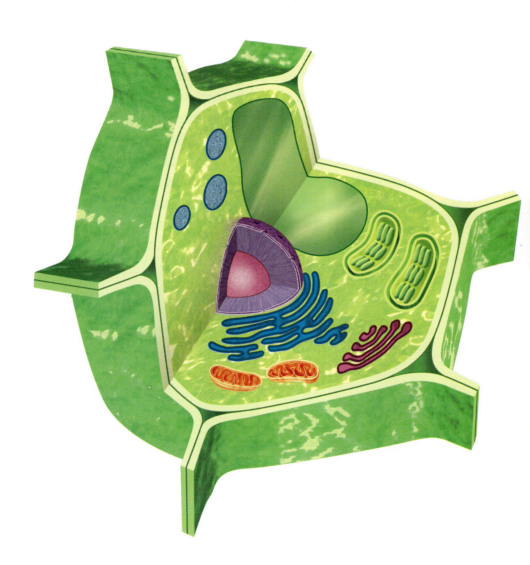

Contents

1

What Are the Parts of a Cell?

Cells are the basic units of living things. Tools called microscopes help scientists learn about the parts of cells and the jobs cells do.

Building Blocks of Life

The simple unit that makes up living things is the cell. All living things are made of cells. Tiny fish, people, and huge elephants are made of cells.

When you look at most living things, you cannot see their cells. That is because most cells are too small to see without a tool called a microscope. The microscope helped scientists discover cells and learn about their parts—or structures.

English scientist Robert Hooke was the first person to study cells with a microscope. He looked at dead cells in a matter called cork. Dutch microscope maker Anton van Leeuwenhoek was the first person to study living cells. He saw tiny living things in a drop of water.

In 1665, Hooke used a microscope to look at thin slices of cork. He saw that the cork was made of many tiny parts that looked like boxes. He called these boxes cells.

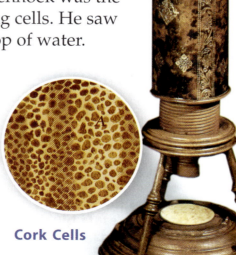

Cork Cells

The Cell Theory

Over time, scientists used stronger microscopes to learn more about cells. In 1838, a German scientist looked at cells from many different plants. He learned that all plants are made of cells. Another scientist learned that all animals are made of cells. Twenty years later, a German doctor learned that cells come only from other cells.

Eventually, these ideas about cells were put together to form one scientific idea, or theory, about cells. This idea is called the cell theory. The cell theory says:

- All living things are made of one or more cells.
- The cell is the smallest unit of a living thing.
- Cells come from other cells.

Microscope Development

The first microscopes had one lens. The lens of a microscope collects and focuses light. Later, two lenses were used to make a compound light microscope. The power of each lens is multiplied together. This makes a compound light microscope much more powerful.

Today's light microscopes can make objects look 2,000 times bigger. That's powerful enough to see structures within cells.

Electron microscopes use quickly moving electrons instead of light to look at objects. They can make objects look 40,000 times bigger.

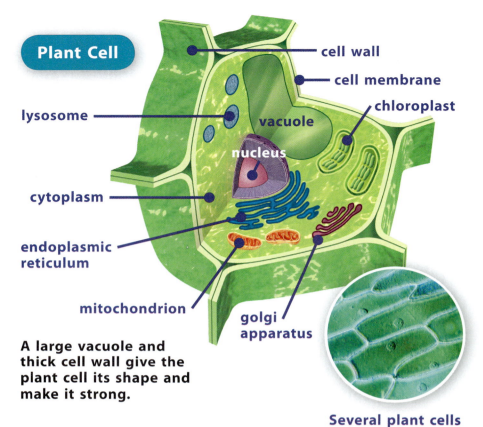

Plant Cell

cell wall

cell membrane

chloroplast

lysosome

vacuole

nucleus

cytoplasm

endoplasmic reticulum

mitochondrion

golgi apparatus

A large vacuole and thick cell wall give the plant cell its shape and make it strong.

Several plant cells

The Parts of a Cell

Cells are made up of structures called <mark>organelles</mark>. Each structure has a job inside the cell. Animal and plant cells have many of the same organelles, but some are very different. As you read about the parts of a cell on the following pages, look for them in the pictures above.

Nucleus The <mark>nucleus</mark> directs what happens in a cell. It holds a tiny bit of matter called DNA. DNA is what makes a living thing have certain traits, or qualities.

Cell Membrane The cell membrane is a thin, bendable cover that is wrapped around all cells. It lets food, water, and gases enter the cell, and it lets wastes leave.

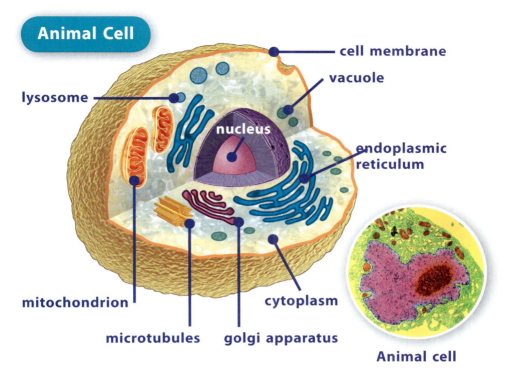

Animal Cell

cell membrane

vacuole

lysosome

nucleus

endoplasmic reticulum

mitochondrion

microtubules

golgi apparatus

cytoplasm

Animal cell

A cell membrane is wrapped around a nucleus and many organelles.

Cell Wall Found only in plant cells, the cell wall is a stiff outer layer around the cell membrane. The cell wall protects the cell and helps a plant stand up. Holes called pores in the cell wall let things pass in and out.

Cytoplasm The cytoplasm is found between the nucleus and the cell membrane. All of the other organelles float in the thick liquid of the cytoplasm.

Ribosomes Tiny ribosomes can be found all over the cell. Ribosomes make proteins. Proteins make up parts of cells and help cells make chemical reactions.

Golgi apparatus The Golgi apparatus takes in proteins and changes them so they are ready to leave the cell.

Lysosomes Lysosomes are small, round organelles that help the cell break down food, or nutrients, and old cell parts. Lysosomes are found in most animal cells, but they are not often found in plant cells.

Vacuoles Vacuoles are sacs filled with liquid. They hold water, food, and waste. Animal cells may have small vacuoles. Plant cells often have one large vacuole.

Mitochondria Mitochondria are large organelles that are shaped like peanuts. They are known as the "power plants" of the cell. Inside the mitochondria, sugars break apart as they mix with oxygen. This action makes carbon dioxide, water, and a lot of energy. Plant and animal cells that need a lot of energy have a lot of mitochondria.

Mitochondrion

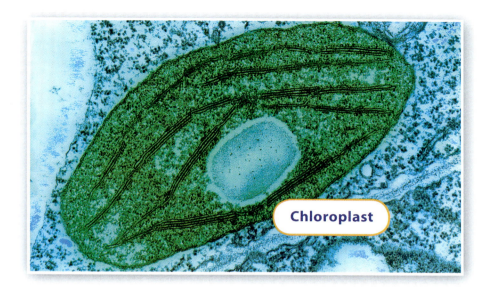

Chloroplast

Chloroplasts Chloroplasts are found mostly in plants. Inside chloroplasts are chemicals called pigments, which take in sunlight. Chloroplasts use this energy to make food. The pigment called chlorophyll gives plants their green color.

Endoplasmic reticulum The endoplasmic reticulum (ER) is a group of membranes and tubes that twist and turn through the cell, forming tunnels. Material moves through the cell in these tunnels. Most cells have two kinds of ER, called rough and smooth. Cells that produce lots of proteins have rough ER that is covered with ribosomes. Smooth ER breaks down deadly matter and controls the amounts of some chemicals. It is not covered by ribosomes.

COMPARE AND CONTRAST

Describe some differences between plant cells and animal cells.

2

How Do Single-Celled Organisms Live?

In single-celled living things, or organisms, all of the actions that are needed for life happen in just one cell.

Life as a Single Cell

All living things have some of the same needs. They need to take in food and get rid of wastes. They need to break down food to use and store energy. They also need to grow and reproduce, or have offspring. These needs are called life processes. Single-celled organisms carry out all of their life processes in one cell.

You can only see most single-celled organisms with a microscope. Because of this, they are also called microorganisms. Bacteria, which can sometimes make you sick, are one kind of microorganism.

The picture below shows a single-celled diatom. The cell is inside a shell. Diatoms live in fresh and salty water. They are an important food eaten by fish and whales.

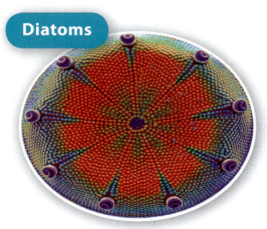

Diatoms

When diatoms die, their shells do not break down. Over time, the shells pile up and form a soft material, like chalk. People use this material to make different kinds of cleaners and many other things. Much of the oil on Earth came from diatoms.

Interactions With Larger Organisms

Single-celled organisms are everywhere. Some are helpful, but some are not.

Helpful single-celled bacteria break down dead animals and plants. They put the material from dead organisms back into the world so new organisms can use it. Bacteria also help to make foods like yogurt and cheese. In fact, your body needs some kinds of bacteria to break down, or digest, foods and to make vitamins.

Other bacteria can make you sick when they enter your body. Antibiotics are medicines that kill harmful bacteria without hurting the good cells in your body.

Algae and yeasts are other helpful single-celled organisms. Like plants, algae give off oxygen, which goes into the air for you to breathe. Yeasts are used to make bread and gasoline.

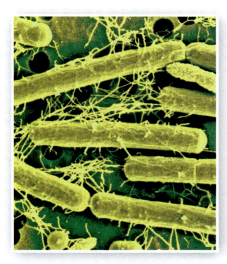

HELPFUL BACTERIA
This type of bacteria is used to make yogurt and cheese.

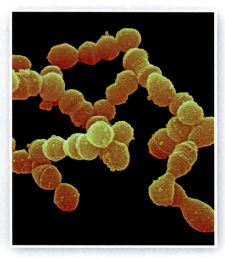

HARMFUL BACTERIA
This type of bacteria can make you sick.

Getting Food

All organisms need energy. Some make their own food. Others take in or eat food from the outside.

Single-celled organisms get food in different ways. An amoeba stretches itself around food, making a bag, or vacuole, around the food. The food is digested in the vacuole and then taken into the cytoplasm.

A paramecium gets food in a different way. Its body has a space called an oral groove. Small hairs called **cilia** move around the opening of the oral groove, pushing pieces of food inside.

At the bottom of the oral groove, a vacuole forms around the food. When the vacuole breaks loose from the oral groove, it carries the food around the cell.

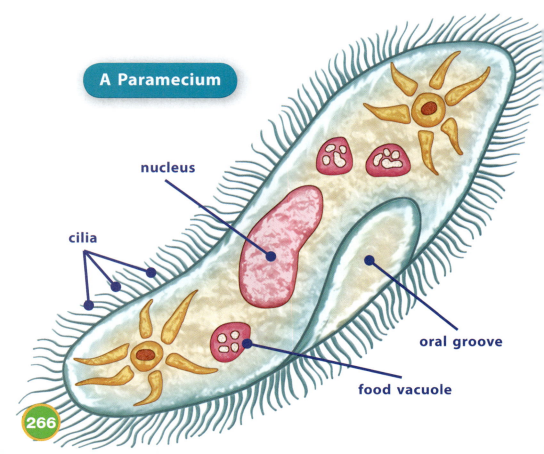

A Paramecium

nucleus

cilia

oral groove

food vacuole

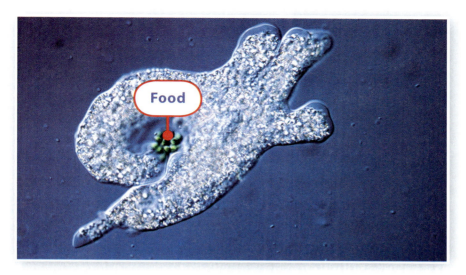

Food

Amoebas use large vacuoles to push extra water out of the cell through the cell membrane. Too much water can harm or kill the cell.

Diffusion

Some things move though the organism's cell membrane. One way this happens is through diffusion. **Diffusion** is the movement of particles from an area crowded with particles to an area where there are fewer particles. **Osmosis** is diffusion in which water passes through the cell membrane.

Too much water flowing into a cell can harm it. Some single-celled organisms also use vacuoles to help control the water. Vacuoles send extra water out through the cell membrane.

Diffusion and osmosis help explain why cells are so small. To stay alive, cells need food, gases, and other things that diffuse through the cell membrane. In a big cell, diffusion could not happen fast enough. The cell membrane would be too small to handle the cell's larger size.

Movement

Some single-celled organisms can move from place to place, like animals do. This is important, because moving allows an organism to find food and a safe place to live, or to escape from enemies, or predators.

The amoeba moves by pushing its cell membrane in front of it. This forms a pseudopod, or "false foot."

The paramecium moves by using its hairy cilia. The cilia move back and forth, like oars on a boat.

Another single-celled organism, the euglena, has a long structure that moves back and forth quickly. This structure is called a **flagellum**. It spins around quickly and moves the euglena forward.

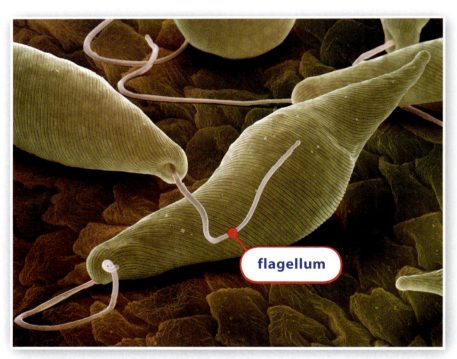

flagellum

Most euglena are green, single-celled organisms that live in ponds. They swim by moving their whip-like structures, called flagella.

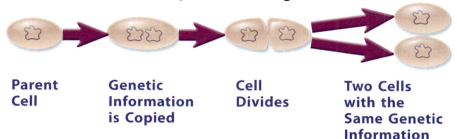

Binary Fission

Bacteria reproduce through fission.

Parent Cell

Genetic Information is Copied

Cell Divides

Two Cells with the Same Genetic Information

Reproduction

Organisms must produce more of their kind so their group of organisms, or species, stays alive. They do this through reproduction. Single-celled organisms reproduce in different ways.

Bacteria reproduce in a simple way called binary fission. Every cell has genetic information— information about itself—inside of it. Before a parent cell reproduces, it grows longer and makes a copy of its genetic information.

Next, the cell breaks apart in the middle to form two new cells. Each piece has the same genetic information inside of it, so the cells will have the same traits, or qualities.

Budding is another type of reproduction. In budding, a small bump, or bud, forms on a parent cell. The bud has the same genetic information as the parent cell. When the bud grows larger, it breaks off of the parent cell. Yeast cells reproduce through budding.

DRAW CONCLUSIONS

Why are bacteria important for all living things?

3

How Do the Cells of Organisms Compare?

Scientists sort, or classify, living things into groups by looking at the things that make them alike and the things that make them different.

Six Kingdoms

You may sort your clothes into separate groups. Perhaps you put socks in one drawer and shirts in another. Sorting things by how they are alike and how they are different is called classification.

Scientists have their own way, or system, of classifying living things. At first, people sorted living things into two groups: plants and animals. But when the microscope was invented, this system did not work as well. Scientists soon learned that many tiny organisms had some traits, or characteristics, of plants and some traits of animals.

Today, scientists classify living things into six groups called kingdoms. A **kingdom** is a large group of organisms with traits that are alike. Three of the six kingdoms are made up mostly of microscopic organisms!

In this picture, you can see organisms from the animal kingdom (squirrel), plant kingdom (moss), and fungi kingdom (mushroom). You cannot see organisms from the protist or bacteria kingdoms, but they are there!

Kingdoms of Life

Kingdom	Cell Characteristics	Other Characteristics
Bacteria (two kingdoms)	single-celled	• live alone or in groups called colonies • cannot move on their own • do not have a nucleus
Protists	mostly single-celled	• live alone or in groups called colonies • some can move on their own, some cannot • some must find food, some make their own food
Fungi	mostly multi-celled	• live alone or in groups called colonies • cannot move on their own • eat living organisms or matter that is breaking down, or decaying
Plants	multi-celled	• have cells with special jobs • do not move from place to place • make their own food using sunlight
Animals	multi-celled	• have cells with special jobs that work together in complex systems • can move on their own • eat organisms from all other kingdoms

Bacteria

Earth is home to many bacteria. The cells of bacteria do not have a nucleus or organelles with membranes around them. Cells like this are called prokaryotic.

There are two bacteria kingdoms: eubacteria and archaebacteria. Most of the bacteria that would be found around you are eubacteria. Archaebacteria are generally found in places such as salty lakes and hot openings along the ocean floor.

Protists

Most **protists** are single-celled, microscopic organisms. Protist cells are eukaryotic, which means they have a nucleus and organelles that are wrapped in membranes. Some protist cells have a cell wall. Some protists can make their own food.

Protozoa (such as amoebas and paramecia), algae (such as diatoms and seaweed), and slime molds are part of the protist kingdom.

This paramecium is a protozoa from the protist kingdom.

Fungi

Most organisms in the fungi kingdom are multicellular, which means they are made of more than one cell. **Fungi** take in food and break down dead plants and animals. Their cells are eukaryotic, so they have organelles and a nucleus. Like plant cells, fungi cells have cell walls, but they do not have chloroplasts.

Fungi come in many shapes and sizes. Microscopic yeasts, molds, and mushrooms are all fungi.

Some fungi are harmful. They can make living things sick and spoil food. Other fungi are eaten as food or are used to make foods and medicines. Fungi are important in nature because they break down dead matter. This makes rich soil that is good for growing plants.

CAP
Spores are kept in the cap until they fall or the wind blows them away.

GILLS
The gills make spores.

STALK
The mushroom stalk holds the cap up so the wind can blow the spores away.

Plants

Plants are multicellular organisms with many parts. They can be tiny mosses or tall trees. Plant cells are eukaryotic, because they have a nucleus and organelles.

Almost all plants use sunlight to make food in a process called photosynthesis. During photosynthesis, organelles called chloroplasts take in energy from sunlight. Plants use that energy to change carbon dioxide and water into sugar and oxygen. Plants, and the animals that eat plants, use the energy in the sugar to live.

All animals need the oxygen that plants make to stay alive. When you breathe, you take in oxygen and breathe out carbon dioxide. Plants take in the carbon dioxide you breathe out and make more oxygen.

Plant cells differ from other cells because they have chloroplasts, a cell wall, and a large vacuole. These structures make plants strong and help them stand up.

Mosses are some of the smallest and most simple plants. They live in wet places and grow near the ground.

Animals

Tiny insects, humans, and huge whales are all part of the animal kingdom. Animals are multicellular organisms with many parts. Most animals can move on their own. All animals do something, or respond, to things like touch or smell. Animals get food by eating other organisms. Animals cannot make food.

One way that scientists sort animals into groups is by separating animals that have internal skeletons, skeletons inside their bodies, from animals that do not.

Animals that do not have internal skeletons or a backbone are called invertebrates. Insects, worms and crabs are invertebrates. Invertebrates have strong muscles or thick outer coverings to hold up their bodies.

Animals with internal skeletons and backbones are called vertebrates. Fish, frogs, and humans are vertebrates. An internal skeleton holds an animal up and protects its organs. There are many more invertebrates than vertebrates.

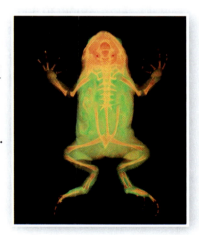

This frog is a vertebrate because it has an internal skeleton.

CLASSIFY

How are bacteria and protists alike? How are they different?

4 How Are Cells Organized?

In multicellular organisms, cells work together to carry out basic life processes, like moving, breathing, and digesting food.

Multicellular Organisms

Multicellular organisms are made up of more than one cell. In these organisms, the cells work together to keep life processes going. The cells are specialized, which means they only do certain jobs. By working together, these cells help an organism stay alive.

Cells come in many shapes and sizes. The shape of a cell often matches the job it does. Nerve cells are long and have many branches, like a tree. This shape helps them take electrical messages, or impulses, all over the body.

Cells in multicellular organisms are sorted, or organized, into different levels. The levels start out simple and get more complex.

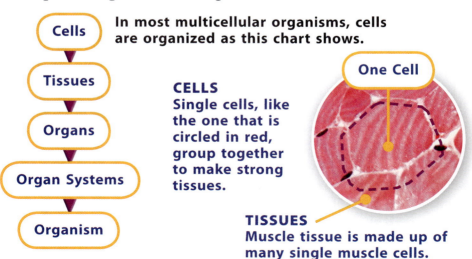

Cells

In most multicellular organisms, cells are organized as this chart shows.

Tissues

Organs

Organ Systems

Organism

CELLS
Single cells, like the one that is circled in red, group together to make strong tissues.

One Cell

TISSUES
Muscle tissue is made up of many single muscle cells.

First, cells are organized into tissues. A **tissue** is a large group of specialized cells that are alike. Tissue comes in many types. Muscle tissue, for example, is made of long groups, or bundles, of muscle cells.

Different types of tissues make up organs. An **organ** is a group of tissues that work together to do a certain job. The heart, brain, and stomach are organs.

Organs are organized into organ systems. An **organ system** is a group of organs that work together to do a certain job. Most multicellular organisms have a number of organ systems that come together to form the total organism. They keep living things alive and healthy.

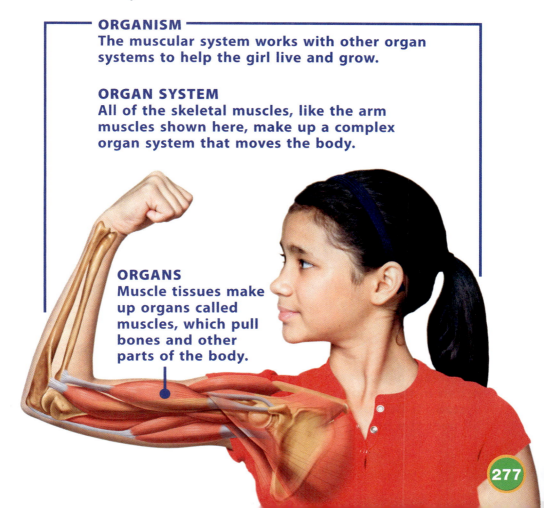

ORGANISM
The muscular system works with other organ systems to help the girl live and grow.

ORGAN SYSTEM
All of the skeletal muscles, like the arm muscles shown here, make up a complex organ system that moves the body.

ORGANS
Muscle tissues make up organs called muscles, which pull bones and other parts of the body.

Circulatory System

The circulatory system is the organ system that brings oxygen and nutrients—things the body needs—to all of the cells in an animal's body. It also takes carbon dioxide and wastes away from the cells.

The heart is the most important organ in the circulatory system. The heart is made of muscle tissue that moves, or pumps, blood. The blood moves through the body in tubes called arteries, veins, and capillaries.

Arteries carry blood away from the heart. Veins carry blood back to the heart. Capillaries are tiny tubes that connect arteries to veins. Capillaries are thin enough to let gases, food, and wastes pass between the blood and body cells.

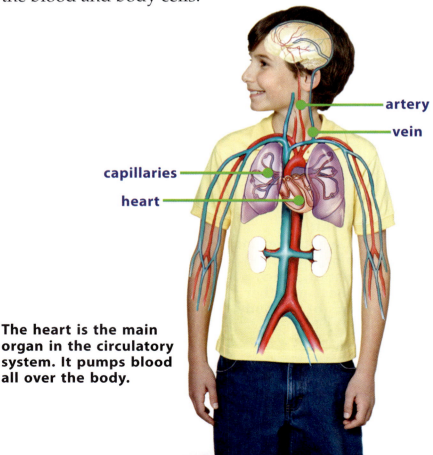

artery

vein

capillaries

heart

The heart is the main organ in the circulatory system. It pumps blood all over the body.

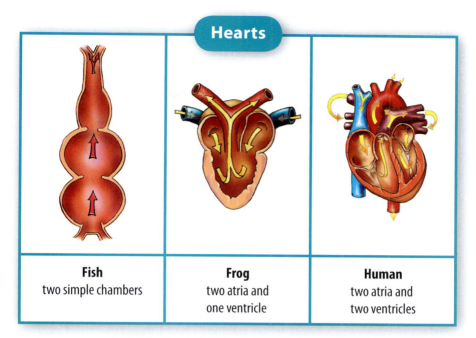

Hearts		
Fish two simple chambers	**Frog** two atria and one ventricle	**Human** two atria and two ventricles

Most animals have some type of heart and circulatory system, but they can be very different. A frog's heart has three chambers instead of four. Fish hearts only have two chambers.

In humans, the heart is divided into four parts called chambers. Veins from the body take blood into a chamber called the right atrium. This blood moves to another chamber, called the right ventricle. From there, it is pumped to the lungs. The blood takes in oxygen from the lungs and leaves carbon dioxide behind.

After moving through the lungs, the blood goes back to the heart and enters the left atrium. It moves through the left atrium into the left ventricle, which is the largest and thickest chamber of the heart. The left ventricle pumps the blood into the arteries. Then the arteries carry the oxygen-rich blood to all parts of the body.

Respiratory System

The respiratory system brings oxygen to the blood and takes carbon dioxide away from it. In humans and other land animals, the lungs are the main organs in the respiratory system.

When you breathe in, air enters your lungs through two tubes called bronchi. Each tube of the bronchi leads to smaller and smaller tubes, ending in little sacs called alveoli.

There are capillaries all around the alveoli. Oxygen passes from the alveoli into the blood. Carbon dioxide passes from the blood into the alveoli.

When you breathe, chest muscles pull your ribs up and down. A muscle called the diaphragm at the bottom of your chest also relaxes and contracts. This makes room for the air that is going in and out of your body.

Different living things have different kinds of respiratory systems. Humans take in air through their noses or mouths. Insects take in air through tiny holes called spiracles. Fish take in oxygen through organs called gills.

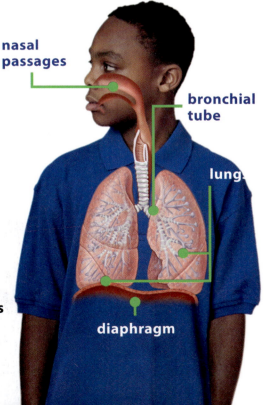

nasal passages

bronchial tube

lungs

diaphragm

Digestive System

The digestive system breaks down, or digests, food so the body can use it. Digestion begins in the mouth, where food is chewed and mixed with liquid called saliva. The food then moves into a tube called the esophagus and on to the stomach.

In the stomach, liquids called gastric fluids and muscles work together to help break down the food more. The food then moves into the small intestine.

Chemicals from the small intestine and from organs called the liver and the pancreas finish breaking down the food. Tiny structures called villi inside the small intestine take in nutrients from the digested food and move them into the blood.

Undigested food and water moves into the large intestine, which takes in most of the water. Any unused material passes out of the body as waste.

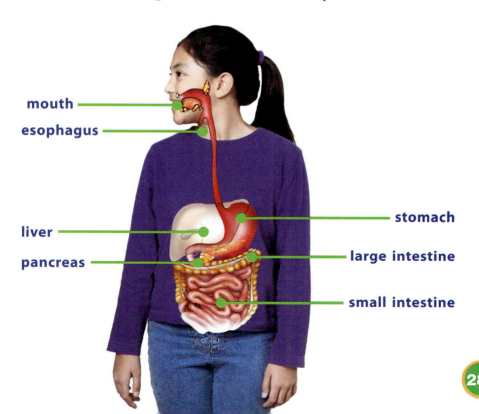

mouth

esophagus

stomach

liver

large intestine

pancreas

small intestine

Nervous System

When you touch hot water, your hand sends a message to your brain. Your brain understands the message and sends a new message to the muscles in your hand to move away from the hot water.

Your nervous system takes in and understands information like this all day, and it controls how the body moves. The specialized cells called neurons that make up the nervous system help the brain do these things.

Neurons take in and send information in little electrical bursts called impulses.

In the brain, more than 100 billion neurons work together to help you think, remember, and learn. A thick string of nerve cells called the spinal cord starts in your brain and moves down your body. Nerves branch out from the spinal cord into your arms and legs. The spinal cord is protected by your backbone.

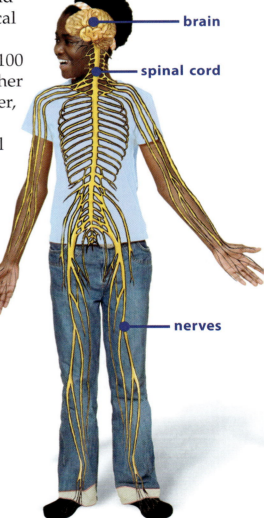

brain

spinal cord

nerves

Muscular and Skeletal System

The muscular system in the human body has three types of muscle tissue:

Smooth Smooth muscles are involuntary muscles. That means you do not have to tell them to contract. These muscles control breathing, the circulation of your blood, and parts of digestion.

Cardiac Cardiac muscle is found only in the heart. It makes your heart beat. It is also an involuntary muscle.

Skeletal Skeletal muscles are voluntary muscles—you must think about moving them before they will move. Skeletal muscles are joined to your bones. They pull on bones and move them. Stringy tissues called ligaments connect bones to bones. Tough tissues called tendons connect bones to muscles. Bones, ligaments, and tendons make up the skeletal system. This system gives your body its shape, lets it move, and protects tissues and organs. Blood cells are also made inside many bones.

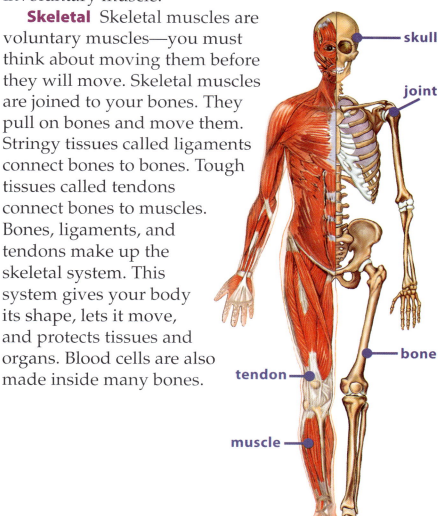

skull

joint

bone

tendon

muscle

Endocrine and Excretory Systems

The endocrine system is made up of glands—organs that send chemical messages called hormones wherever the body needs them. Each hormone that your body makes works with one kind of cell.

Endocrine glands are all over the body. One kind of endocrine gland is your thyroid gland, which is in your neck. It controls the way your cells make and use energy. The excretory system uses the large intestine and kidneys to take wastes out of your body and control your body's water levels. Kidneys are organs near the middle of your back. They take waste and extra water out of your blood, moving them into the bladder and out of your body. Without this system, wastes would make you sick.

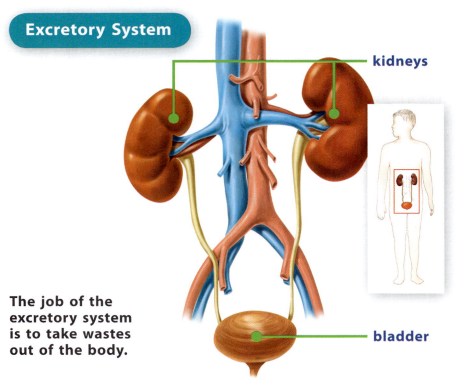

Excretory System

kidneys

bladder

The job of the excretory system is to take wastes out of the body.

Other Systems

The human body has many other organ systems. For example, the lymphatic system moves liquid called lymph all through your body. Lymph keeps extra water out of your tissues.

Skin, fingernails, and hair are all part of the integumentary system. The immune system protects your body from bacteria and other things that can make you sick. It makes antibodies, or proteins that help fight diseases, and moves them through your blood.

All body systems work together in many ways. For example, when you run, your nerves and muscles work together to move your skeletal system. Nerves tell your heart to pump faster and slow down your digestive system. Most of these things happen without you even thinking about it!

Your Organ Systems

Endocrine System

Circulatory System

Respiratory System

Digestive System

Nervous System

Excretory System

Muscular System

Skeletal System

Keeping Healthy

There are many simple things you can do to stay healthy. To kill bacteria that can make you sick, wash your hands often. Always cover your mouth and nose if you cough or sneeze. This will help stop the spread of bacteria to other people.

Eating fresh foods that have many vitamins gives cells the nutrients they need. Choosing not to smoke or use drugs keeps cells strong so they can fight off sickness. Being active keeps your muscles in good shape. It also helps you breathe better and helps your body processes run smoothly.

Doctors can look at x-ray pictures to see some of your organs.

MAIN IDEA AND DETAILS

What is an organ system?

Glossary

cell (sehl), the basic structural unit of a living thing

cilia (SIHL ee uh), small structures that look like hairs

diffusion (dih FYOO zhuhn), movement of particles from an area of higher concentration to an area of lower concentration

flagellum (fluh JEHL uhm), whip-like tail that helps single-celled organisms move by spinning like a propeller

fungi (FUHN jee), kingdom of living things; its organisms are multicellular, have nuclei, and often feed on decaying matter

kingdom (KIHNG duhm), largest group of organisms that share traits in common

nucleus (NOO klee uhs), storehouse of the cell's most important chemical information, or the central core of an atom

Glossary

organ (AWR guhn), group of one or more kinds of tissues that work together to perform the same function

organ system (AWR guhn SIHS tuhm), group of interconnected organs that perform related life functions

organelle (AWR guh nehl), cell structure that performs specific functions

osmosis (ahz MOH sihs), type of diffusion in which water passes through a cell membrane

protist (PROH tihst), kingdom of living things; its organisms are mostly one-celled but have nuclei and other organelles

tissue (TIHSH oo), group of one or more kinds of specialized cells that perform the same function

Think About What You Have Read

Vocabulary

❶ Which kingdom is made mostly of single-celled eukaryotes?

A) eubacteria

B) archaebacteria

C) protists

D) fungi

Comprehension

❷ What are the three main points of the cell theory?

❸ What do the terms diffusion and osmosis mean?

❹ What are the six kingdoms into which living things are classified?

Critical Thinking

❺ What other body systems does the circulatory system affect? Describe the jobs the circulatory system has in the body.

Plant Systems

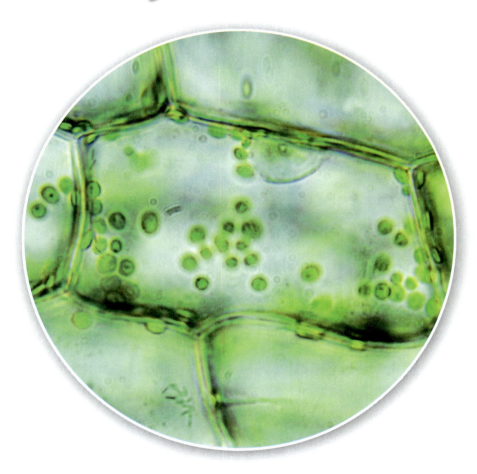

Contents

1 How Do Plants Make Food?

Plants use energy from the Sun to make food. They mix carbon dioxide and water to make sugar. At the same time, they give off oxygen.

Photosynthesis

You use energy all the time. You need energy for all of your life processes, such as sleeping, breathing, moving, and thinking.

The energy you use really comes from the Sun. Remember that plants change the energy of sunlight into chemical energy that is stored in food. Plants do this through a process called **photosynthesis**.

During photosynthesis, plants mix water and carbon dioxide to make sugars. They also give off oxygen. Sugars are a plant's food. The plant stores sugars in its tissues and breaks them down when it needs energy.

Plants like this vine use photosynthesis to make food.

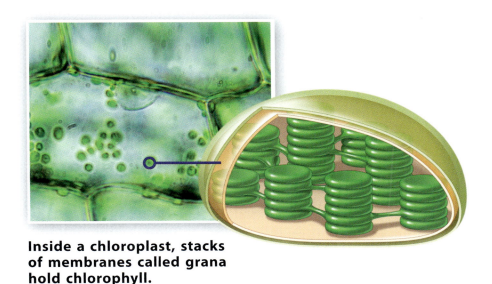

Inside a chloroplast, stacks
of membranes called grana
hold chlorophyll.

When an animal eats the plant, the animal can use
the plant's sugars as energy. And when a larger animal
eats the plant-eater, it also gets energy that was first
stored in plants. This is how all animals get their
energy from plants.

Photosynthesis happens in organelles called
chloroplasts. The number of chloroplasts in a cell is
different for different organisms. Some tiny algae cells
have only one chloroplast. The cells in the leaves of a
tree may each have more than fifty chloroplasts.

Most chloroplasts are put together in the same way.
There are two thin coverings, or membranes, around
each one. Another group of membranes moves
through the inside of the chloroplast. These
membranes look like flat bags that are stacked on top
of each other. They are called grana.

Inside these membranes are different pigments.
Pigments absorb, or take in, light. The most important
pigment in a chloroplast is chlorophyll.

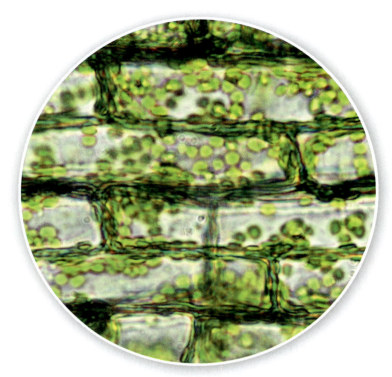

All plants and animals use energy that is made in tiny plant cells.

Sunlight is made up of many different colors. Chlorophyll absorbs most colors of light, but not green. This means that when sunlight hits chlorophyll, green light is sent back to your eye. This is why plant parts that have a lot of chlorophyll look green.

How does photosynthesis work? When light hits chlorophyll, the energy is used to break apart water molecules into hydrogen and oxygen. Chemical changes make the hydrogen join with carbon from carbon dioxide to form sugars. The oxygen is let go.

It is hard to imagine life on Earth without photosynthesis. When you look at a tall tree or other plant, remember that almost all of its matter came from only water and carbon dioxide.

Plant Leaves

In almost all plants, leaves hold most of the chloroplasts. A plant's food is made inside leaves. You can think of leaves as a plant's "food factory!"

Plant leaves come in many different shapes and sizes. They can be round or shaped like a heart. They can be smooth or have bumpy or sharp edges.

The wide, flat part of a leaf is called the blade. Scientists sort leaves into groups by looking at their blades. A simple leaf has a blade that is just one piece. Oak trees and apple trees have simple leaves. A compound leaf has a blade that is separated into parts. Rose bushes and palm trees have compound leaves.

Leaves are made of different tissues. The outside layer of leaf tissue is called the epidermis. The cells in this tissue have a waterproof covering that keeps the water inside the cells.

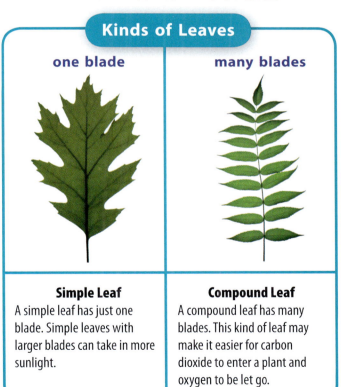

Kinds of Leaves

one blade

many blades

Simple Leaf
A simple leaf has just one blade. Simple leaves with larger blades can take in more sunlight.

Compound Leaf
A compound leaf has many blades. This kind of leaf may make it easier for carbon dioxide to enter a plant and oxygen to be let go.

Plants need to take in and send out gases. Small holes in the epidermis let gases move in and out of the plant cells. These holes are called **stomata**. Stomata are found on the bottom side of the leaf.

Specialized plant parts act like gates by opening and closing the stomata. When the stomata open, carbon dioxide goes in, and oxygen and water vapor go out.

Stomata often open in daylight, during photosynthesis. At night, stomata generally close to keep water in the leaf. Stomata also may stay closed during dry or hot weather to save water.

Most of the cells that help with photosynthesis can be found just below the epidermis. These cells have plenty of air in between them so gases can move easily.

Long, thin tubes called veins are also found in leaves. Veins carry things in and out of the leaf. They connect the leaf's cells to the rest of the plant.

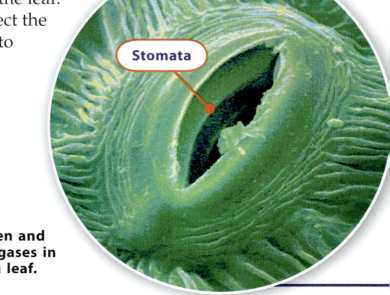

Stomata

Stomata open and close to let gases in and out of a leaf.

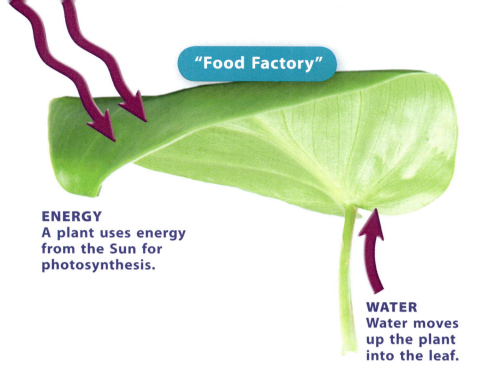

"Food Factory"

ENERGY
A plant uses energy from the Sun for photosynthesis.

WATER
Water moves up the plant into the leaf.

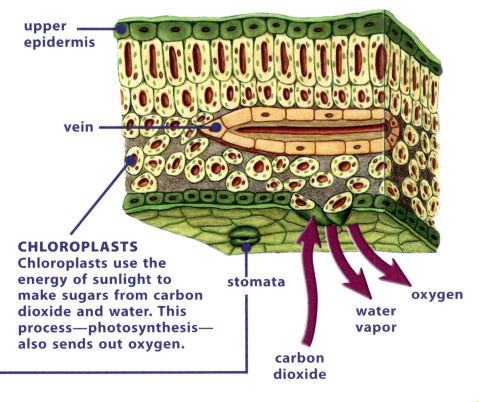

upper epidermis

vein

CHLOROPLASTS
Chloroplasts use the energy of sunlight to make sugars from carbon dioxide and water. This process—photosynthesis—also sends out oxygen.

stomata

oxygen

water vapor

carbon dioxide

Carbon and Oxygen Cycles

Why is there always enough oxygen in the air? Why doesn't the air fill up with carbon dioxide? The reason is that oxygen and carbon dioxide cycle, or keep moving, through the world around us.

Plants take in carbon dioxide and give off oxygen. Both plants and animals use oxygen to break down sugars. As they break down sugars, they send out carbon dioxide. Together, plants and animals reuse the gases they both need, over and over.

Some things people do can cause problems for the carbon and oxygen cycles. Fossil fuels are fuels that come from dead plant and animal matter. They hold stored carbon inside of them. When people burn fossil fuels such as coal, oil, and natural gas, the carbon is sent out as carbon dioxide.

Animals and plants need each other to keep the carbon and oxygen cycles working well.

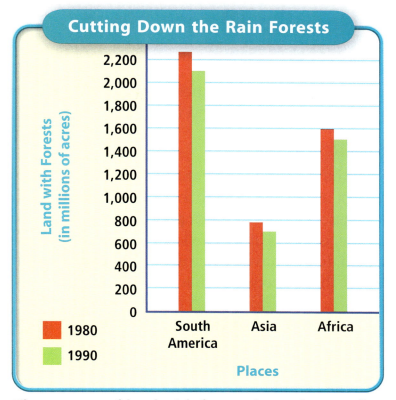

Cutting Down the Rain Forests

Land with Forests (in millions of acres)

2,200
2,000
1,800
1,600
1,400
1,200
1,000
800
600
400
200
0

■ 1980
■ 1990

South America   Asia   Africa

Places

The amount of land with forests is getting smaller all over the world.

Today people are burning fossil fuels very quickly. This sends a lot of carbon into the air. People are also cutting down trees in forests. Large parts of rain forests in South America and other places have been cut down. This means that there are fewer trees to take carbon out of the air and send oxygen into the air.

SEQUENCE

What happens during the process of photosynthesis?

2 How Do Plants Move Materials?

Plants have specialized tissues and use natural forces to move water, minerals, and food.

Nonvascular Plants

If you have ever looked at fuzzy moss growing on the side of a tree, you know that not all plants look alike. Mosses are **nonvascular plants.** They do not have structures, or parts, like true leaves, stems, or roots. They also do not have structures to move food, water, and other things between plant parts.

Liverworts and hornworts are also nonvascular plants. They have very few specialized cells, cells that do a certain job. They also have no complex organs.

Nonvascular plants are almost always small because they cannot move water very far. Most of the cells of nonvascular plants must be close to the world outside them. This lets gases, water, and minerals move between the outside world and the cells.

Even though they are small, nonvascular plants are important. By taking in water, they help hold soil in place and keep it from getting too dry.

liverwort

moss

This sunflower is a vascular plant.

Vascular Plants

Most plants you can name, including evergreen trees, flowers, and ferns, are vascular plants. A <mark>vascular plant</mark> has specialized tissues that move materials through the plant. Veins carry materials in and out of the leaves. Veins are vascular tissues.

Three of the organs of vascular plants are roots, stems, and leaves. Roots hold a plant in the ground. They also take in water and minerals from the soil. Some roots also store food for the plant.

The stem helps a plant stand up and holds its leaves up in the air so they can take in sunlight. Water, minerals, and food also move from the roots to the leaves through the stem. The trunk of a tree is the tree's main stem.

Stems are made of two important kinds of tissues: xylem and phloem. **Xylem** tissues move water and minerals up from the roots. **Phloem** tissues move food materials down from the leaves to the rest of the plant.

Most plant stems have a ring of bundles that are made of both xylem and phloem. A strip of tissue called the vascular cambium lies between the xylem and phloem. This is where xylem and phloem cells are made.

Tree Trunk

phloem   xylem

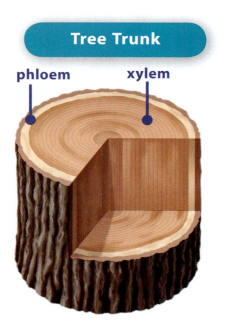

Stem

xylem

vascular cambium

phloem

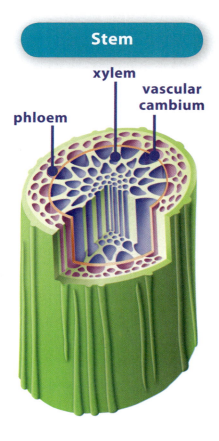

The Upward Flow of Water

Most of the time, water flows downward. But in the stems of plants, water flows upward because of root pressure, cohesion, and transpiration.

Water enters the roots because roots are dryer than the soil around them. Specialized cells in the roots hold the water in. As the roots fill with water, a force called pressure gets stronger and starts to push the water up the plant.

Water molecules stick together because of a force called cohesion. They also stick to other things because of a force called adhesion. These forces move water farther up the tubes of xylem tissue.

To reach the tops of taller plants, water needs the pull of transpiration. During transpiration, evaporation occurs throughout the leaves of a plant. As water moves out of the plant leaves into the air, more water is pulled through the plant to take its place.

Transpiration pulls water up through the stem.

Cohesion forces water up the tubes of xylem tissue.

Root pressure pushes water and minerals upward.

TEXT STRUCTURE

What are two types of vascular tissue?

3 How Do Plants Reproduce?

Plants reproduce using spores or seeds. The spores and seeds are moved in different ways.

Seedless Plants and Conifers

The path a plant follows as it begins life, grows, and reproduces is called its life cycle. Scientists sort plants into two major groups by looking at their life cycles. One group is the seed plants, which reproduce with seeds. The other group is the seedless plants, which reproduce with **spores** or other structures. Ferns are seedless plants that reproduce with spores.

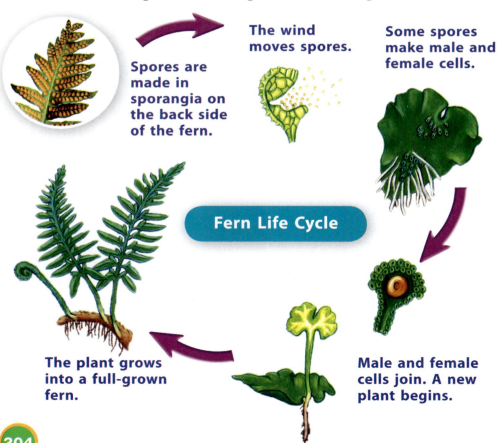

Spores are made in sporangia on the back side of the fern.

The wind moves spores.

Some spores make male and female cells.

Fern Life Cycle

The plant grows into a full-grown fern.

Male and female cells join. A new plant begins.

male cone

Male pine cones make pollen. Female pine cones make ovules. Seeds develop in the female cones.

female cone

Most large plants are seed plants. Scientists sort seed plants into two large groups: gymnosperms and angiosperms. Plants with seeds that are not hidden inside of fruit are called **gymnosperms**. Plants called conifers, such as pine trees, are common gymnosperms. Conifer seeds grow inside cones.

Conifers make male and female cones, sometimes both on the same plant. Male cones make pollen, a material that has male gametes, or sperm cells, which are used for reproduction. Female cones, called seed cones, have ovules. Ovules hold female gametes, or eggs.

In the spring, pollen cones send out pollen into the wind. Some of the pollen is blown onto seed cones. When pollen is delivered to eggs, the process is called **pollination**.

When pollen lands on a seed cone, it lets go of sperm cells, which fertilize the ovules. This forms a zygote, which will turn into seeds. When the seeds are ready, they fall from the cone and can grow into new conifers.

Flower Life Cycle

GERMINATION Germination takes place when a seed begins to grow as a new plant.

FRUITS
Fruits are mature plant ovaries. Fruits get bigger to protect and feed seeds.

FERTILIZATION Fertilization takes place inside the ovary, when a male gamete from the pollen joins a female gamete in the ovary.

Flowering Plants

The second large group of seed plants is called angiosperms. **Angiosperms** are also called flowering plants because their seeds are protected inside flowers and fruits. Most of the plants in the world are flowering plants. Flowers are the organs angiosperms use for reproduction. They have many parts.

The male reproductive organ is called a stamen. The stamen has a thin stalk and a rounded anther. The anther makes pollen.

The female reproductive organ of a flower is called a pistil. The pistil has three parts: the stigma, the style, and the ovary. The stigma is the sticky tip of the pistil. The style joins the stigma and the ovary. The ovary holds the ovules. Not all flowering plants make both male and female reproductive organs in the same flower.

The colorful parts of a flower that look like leaves are called petals. They protect the flower's reproductive organs.

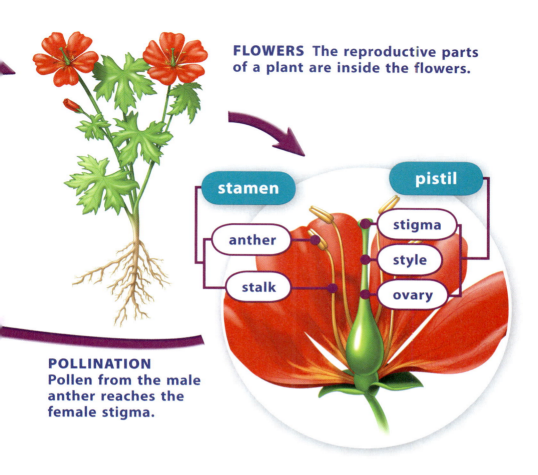

FLOWERS The reproductive parts of a plant are inside the flowers.

stamen

anther

stalk

pistil

stigma

style

ovary

POLLINATION Pollen from the male anther reaches the female stigma.

In flowering plants, pollination happens soon after a tiny bit of pollen lands on the sticky stigma. If the pollen is from the right kind of plant, the pollen makes a tube that grows through the style and into the ovule. A sperm cell is sent out of the tube to fertilize the egg cell inside the ovule. A zygote grows and turns into a seed that might someday grow into a new plant.

As the seed grows, the ovary changes into a fruit. The fruit keeps the seed safe and gives it food so it can grow. Fruits like apples, oranges, cherries, and berries are ovaries that grow around the seeds inside them. Foods such as tomatoes, peppers, and cucumbers are ovaries, too.

Pollination

Pollen can be moved in many ways. Here are some examples.

Self-pollination In plants such as beans and peas, pollen moves from the male parts to the female parts on the same flower.

Wind Some plants, like corn, send pollen into the wind. Plants that need the wind for pollination often have parts such as long stamens that raise the pollen into the open air. They may also have stigma with fluffy arms that catch pollen from the air.

Water Some plants, such as sea grasses, live in water and use water to carry pollen. The bits of pollen float from male parts to female parts.

Animals Flowers with bright colors or strong smells are generally pollinated by animals that come to eat the sweet liquid in the flower. As these animals, such as bees and butterflies, rest on the flowers, pollen sticks to their bodies. The animals then move the pollen to other flowers.

Pollen sticks to the thick leg hairs of honeybees.

**Each burr on this dog holds seeds.
The dog helps spread them around.**

Moving Seeds Around

Like pollen, plant seeds can be moved in many ways.

Wind Some plants, like dandelions, have small, light seeds that can be carried by the wind.

Water Some plant seeds and fruits can be moved by water. These fruits and seeds have air inside of them to help them float in the water.

Animals Burrs are fruits that stick to the fur of animals. As an animal moves around, it carries the seeds to new places.

Many animals like eating sweet fruits. As an animal eats the fruit, some of the seeds may drop to the ground, where they may grow into new plants.

Animals that eat fruit also help spread seeds in another way. Some seeds pass through the body of an animal without being broken down. They are part of the animal's waste. Birds that eat fruit often spread plant seeds this way.

Many Kinds of Flowering Plants

Angiosperms grow in most places on Earth. A few kinds of angiosperms even live in ocean water. Angiosperms around the world have many kinds of structures that help them reproduce in the places they live.

Flowers come in many different shapes, sizes, and colors. Water lilies have some of the largest flowers. Grasses and clover have some of the smallest. The most common flower colors are red, yellow, white, and blue.

Fruits also come in many sizes. Tiny berries and large coconuts are both fruits. Fruits grow around different kinds and numbers of seeds. Strawberries have many tiny seeds. A grape or apple might have two or three seeds. Cherries or avocados have only one seed.

People have grown and enjoyed many kinds of fruits, flowers, and seeds for thousands of years. People even eat some flowers, such as broccoli!

Some flowers live in the water, such as these water lilies.

Look at the chart below to see how flowers, fruits, and seeds can be different.

Comparing Flowering Plants

Grasses
- many small flowers grouped together
- flowers can be put together in many different ways

Avocado
- soft fruit
- one large seed
- seed inside of the fruit

Sunflower
- head is made up of many small flowers
- each flower makes one seed

Orange
- soft fruit
- many small seeds
- seeds in the center of the fruit

Corn
- groups of male flowers called tassels
- female flowers are inside the ears of corn
- corn grains are made by female flowers

Strawberry
- soft fruit
- many tiny seeds
- seeds spread all over the outside of the fruit

COMPARE AND CONTRAST

What are different ways that pollen and seeds are moved around?

Glossary

angiosperms (AN jee uh spurmz), plants with seeds covered by protective fruits

chlorophyll (KLAWR uh fihl), the green pigment in leaves that collects energy from sunlight

chloroplasts (KLAWR uh plast), plant organelles inside which photosynthesis takes place

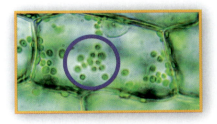

gymnosperms (JIHM nuh spurmz), plants with seeds that are not covered by protective fruits

nonvascular plant (nahn VAS kyoo luhr plant), a simple plant that lacks true leaves, stems, and roots

phloem (FLOH ehm), specialized tissue within roots, stems, and leaves that moves materials

photosynthesis (foh toh SIHN thih sihs), the process by which plants use light energy to convert water and carbon dioxide into sugars and oxygen

Glossary

pollination (pahl ih NAY shuhn), process of delivering pollen (male) to the egg (female) in a plant

spores (spawrz), reproductive structures found in fungi and simple plants

stomata (STOH muh tuh), small openings through which gases move in and out of leaves

transpiration (tran spuh RAY shuhn), evaporation through the leaves of a plant

vascular plant (VAS kyoo luhr plant), a plant with specialized tissues and organs for transporting materials

xylem (ZY luhm), specialized plant tissue that moves materials

Think About What You Have Read

Vocabulary

❶ Angiosperms produce their gametes inside _____ .

A) flowers

B) sporangia

C) cones

D) stems

Comprehension

❷ What are the two main products of photosynthesis?

❸ How do forces push and pull materials through a plant?

❹ What do sporangia, cones, and flowers have in common? How are they different?

Critical Thinking

❺ Why do moss plants grow best in damp places, such as the floor of a forest? Would mosses grow well in dry, sandy soil? Explain.

Ecosystems, Communities, and Biomes

Contents

1

How Do Living Things Form Communities?

An ecosystem is a community of different plants and animals. It also includes water, soil, and other nonliving things.

What Is an Ecosystem?

If you put your head on the ground in a forest, what would you see? You might see ants or worms. Twigs and leaves might stick in your hair.

The ground in the forest is one kind of ecosystem. An **ecosystem** is made up of all the living and nonliving things that interact in one place. In a forest, the living things might be very small or very large. Plants and animals are living things. Some nonliving things are sunlight, soil, water, and air.

An ecosystem can be small, such as a rotting log or a patch of soil under a tree. It can also be large, such as a forest or a prairie. The size does not matter. Everything in an ecosystem interacts.

Soil, a log, moss, and a lizard are part of this small ecosystem.

The Florida Everglades is a large ecosystem. The land is swampy, covered by a layer of muddy water. Grasses grow tall because only a few trees block the sunlight.

Near the ocean, salt water mixes with the fresh water. Mangrove trees grow in these areas. Fish and shrimp are found there, too. Many birds nest in the mangroves. They eat the fish and shrimp.

The birds, fish, and trees in the Everglades are part of a community. A **community** is the group of living things found in an ecosystem. These living things depend on one another for food, shelter, and other needs. They also depend on nonliving things. Some living things in an ecosystem might not be able to survive in a different ecosystem.

The Florida Everglades is an ecosystem with many living and nonliving things.

Populations

A **population** consists of all the members of the same type of organism that live in an ecosystem.

The Everglades ecosystem has populations of trees, alligators, spoonbills, and many others. The birth or death of one plant or animal will probably not change the Everglades very much. But what would happen if all the mangrove trees died? An event like this can affect the entire community.

Scientists study ecosystems. They think about things that affect the whole community. One major part of the Everglades ecosystem is the water supply. Living things in the Everglades depend on fresh water. But humans need the water, too. Their needs are growing every year. They are draining the supply.

MAIN IDEA

How do scientists classify the parts of an ecosystem?

Roseate spoonbill

Alligator

2

What Are Biomes?

Biomes are large regions of Earth. Each biome has a certain kind of climate. Different communities of living things are found in different climates.

Earth's Major Biomes

A **biome** is a large group of ecosystems that are the same in some ways. The map below shows six main land biomes.

What makes biomes different from one another? The most important thing is climate. **Climate** is the kind of weather that occurs in a place over a long time. Some climates are rainy. Some are very dry. Some have hot and cold weather. Others are almost always hot or always cold. Different climates have different populations of living things.

Earth has six major land biomes.

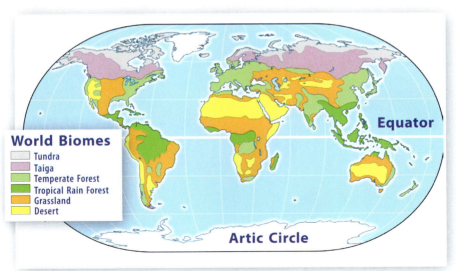

World Biomes
- Tundra
- Taiga
- Temperate Forest
- Tropical Rain Forest
- Grassland
- Desert

Equator

Artic Circle

Forest Biomes

Forest biomes have tall trees. Animals live in the trees and on the ground. Forests are part of two biomes. The first kind of forest biome is a tropical rain forest. **Tropical rain forests** are very rainy and hot. Some rain forests get more than 600 cm (240 in.) of rain each year! Temperatures are between 18°C and 35°C (64°F to 95°F). This makes it like summer all year.

Tropical rain forests have many living things. Many different kinds of plants and animals live in this biome. Plants in rain forests make much of Earth's oxygen. Some of these plants might be used to make products to help people.

Tropical Rain Forest

Location: near the equator

Climate: warm and wet

The other kind of forest biome is a temperate forest. **Temperate forests** have four different seasons: summer, fall, winter, and spring. Temperatures can be as cold as –30°C (–22°F) or as warm as 30°C (86°F). A temperate forest gets about one-fifth the rainfall of a tropical rain forest.

Temperate forests have animals such as deer, rabbits, skunks, squirrels, and bears. Trees in these forests lose their leaves in the fall. The leaves fall on the ground and rot. This makes the soil richer. The trees stay alive through the winter, but they do not grow during that time.

Temperate Forest

Location: North America and other places

Climate: four different seasons

Grasslands and Deserts

The land in the **grasslands** biome is covered with grasses. There are very few trees. Most grasslands have a dry season, which is a long time without rain.

There are two main kinds of grasslands: prairies and savannas. Prairies are found where the climate is mild. Temperatures may drop to –40°C (–40°F) in winter. They may rise to 38°C (100°F) in summer. Prairie animals include prairie dogs, coyotes, and hawks.

Most savannas are found in warm places. Temperatures may remain above 18°C (64°F) all year. Elephants, lions, and zebras live on a savanna.

Grasslands

Location: central Africa, central United States, and other places

Climate: has a dry season

The **desert** is the driest biome. Most deserts get less than 25 cm (10 in.) of rain each year. Some deserts may not get any rain for a whole year. Deserts may be cold or hot.

Desert plants and animals have features that help them live with little water. For example, a cactus has a waxy coating and spiny leaves. This helps it hold water. Earth's driest deserts contain little life. Many are filled with sandy dunes that stretch for miles and miles.

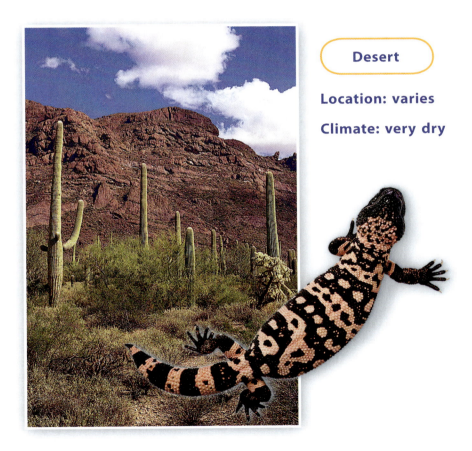

Desert

Location: varies

Climate: very dry

Taiga and Tundra

The <mark>taiga</mark> biome has long, harsh winters and short, cool summers. Temperatures reach 10°C (50°F) only a few months each year. The taiga is dry. It gets about 40 cm (20 in.) of precipitation each year, mostly snow.

Most of the trees in the taiga are pines, firs, and spruces. The leaves of these trees are thin, waxy needles. This helps the trees hold water. Their leaves do not fall all at once when the weather turns cold. Moose, deer, and wolves live in the taiga.

Taiga

Location: in the far north

Climate: long cold winters and short cool summers

The taiga's climate is mild compared to the tundra. The **tundra** is Earth's coldest biome. It has an average temperature of −34°C (−29°F). The ground is frozen for many layers under the surface. The lower layers stay frozen all year long. These layers are called permafrost.

In summer, temperatures are only about 10°C (50°F). As the ground thaws, the tundra becomes swampy. Mosses and small trees grow. There are many mosquitoes.

Polar bears and reindeer live in the tundra. These animals have features that help them live in the cold. For example, polar bears have a thick layer of fat to keep them warm.

Tundra

Location: near the Arctic Circle

Climate: very, very cold

Marine Biomes

Oceans cover 70 percent of Earth. In the oceans are marine biomes. There are three zones, or parts, to marine biomes.

The first zone is the intertidal zone. Living things have features to help them live on or near the ocean shore. Near land, the water level changes with the tides. Ocean tides cover and uncover the land. Sometimes the land is under water. Sometimes it is in the Sun and air.

In this zone, some animals can stick to rocks so the waves won't wash them away. Other animals can move in land or water.

Intertidal Zone

Near-Shore Zone

Some animals live where water levels change over and over.

Some fish live among kelp in places where the water is not very deep.

The second zone is the near-shore zone. Tall, brown plants called kelp live in the water here. Some animals live among the kelp.

The third zone is far out in the ocean. It is called the open ocean zone. The water here is deep and cold. Tiny algae float on top of the water. Algae are like plants. There are many algae. They make most of Earth's oxygen! They are also food for ocean animals.

Sunlight does not go far down into the water. So, the deepest part of the ocean is very cold and dark. Animals that live here have features to help them live. For example, some fish make their own light. The light helps them hunt for food.

Large schools of fish live in the open ocean zone.

Open Ocean Zone

Some fish live in cold and dark water deep in the ocean. They may look very different from other fish.

Freshwater Ecosystems

Many bodies of water are made up of fresh water. Streams, rivers, ponds, lakes, and wetlands are freshwater ecosystems.

Streams and rivers contain water that moves, or flows. Near the start of a river, this flow is almost always fast. The water is clear. Fish that can swim fast live in this part of the river. Later, the flow slows and the river gets wider. Plants can take root in the muddy bottom. Fish, beavers, and many birds may live here.

As the river flows, it picks up small rocks and dirt. Near the mouth, or end, of the river it drops the rocks and dirt. The water here is dark. Other kinds of fish may live here.

Some birds hunt for fish in fresh water.

Ponds and lakes have water that does not flow. Some are small. Others are very large. Deep ponds and lakes have three different areas. Algae, plants, insects, and fish live near the top. They need the warmth and light of the Sun. Farther down the water is cooler. Some sunlight shines through. Tiny living things called plankton live here. Many animals eat plankton.

Near the bottom is a deep, cold area. Few things live here. Tiny living things called bacteria break down dead plants and animals.

TEXT STRUCTURE

Compare the conditions in the three zones of the ocean.

Many plants and animals live in freshwater ecosystems.

3

What Is a Food Web?

In an ecosystem, energy flows from producers to consumers to decomposers.

Energy from Food

A producer makes its own food. Plants are Earth's producers. They make food from air and water, and energy. Algae and some kinds of bacteria are producers, too.

Plants and other producers use energy from the Sun. They change it into a different kind of energy. Plants make sugars and oxygen. They use some of these sugars to grow. They store the rest.

A consumer does not produce food. A consumer gets energy by eating food. When you eat a plant, you take in the energy stored in the plant. Humans and all other animals are consumers.

Producer
Grass and plants are producers.

First-Level Consumer
The caterpillar is a consumer that eats leaves.

Second-Level Consumer
The bird eats the caterpillar.

Food Chains

A **food chain** shows how energy in an ecosystem moves from one living thing to another.

Almost all food chains begin with the Sun. Producers use the Sun's energy to make food. Animals that eat plants or other producers are called first-level consumers.

Some consumers eat other consumers. Birds are second-level consumers. They eat very small consumers. Cats are third-level consumers. They eat larger consumers than birds do. However, all consumers rely on plants. Without plants, there would not be a food chain.

When plants and animals die, sometimes they are eaten. Sometimes decomposers break down the parts. Bacteria and worms are two kinds of decomposers. They make the dead plants and animals part of the soil.

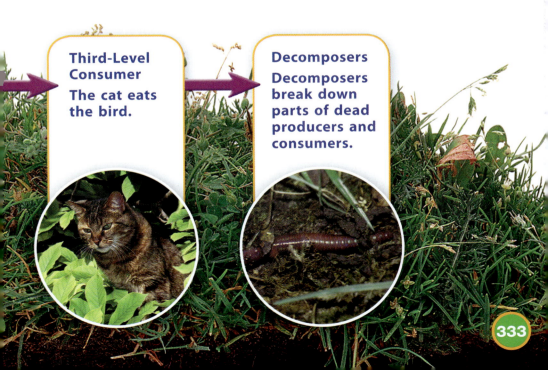

Third-Level Consumer

The cat eats the bird.

Decomposers

Decomposers break down parts of dead producers and consumers.

Food Webs

A **food web** shows how food chains work in an ecosystem. Look at the food web on page 19. The plants are producers. The mouse eats plant seeds. It also eats insects. The snake eats insects, too. But it also eats mice. The hawk eats mice and snakes. So does the fox.

Classifying Consumers Most consumers play the same role in every food chain they are part of. For example, a rabbit is always a first-level consumer. It is an herbivore, which means "plant eater."

Other consumers are called carnivores, which means "meat eaters." Hawks and snakes are examples of carnivores. Some carnivores are second-level consumers. Some are third-level consumers. Many carnivores hunt and kill other animals.

Some animals eat both plants and animals. They are omnivores, which means "eats all." Bears are omnivores. If you eat both plant and animal products, you are an omnivore, too.

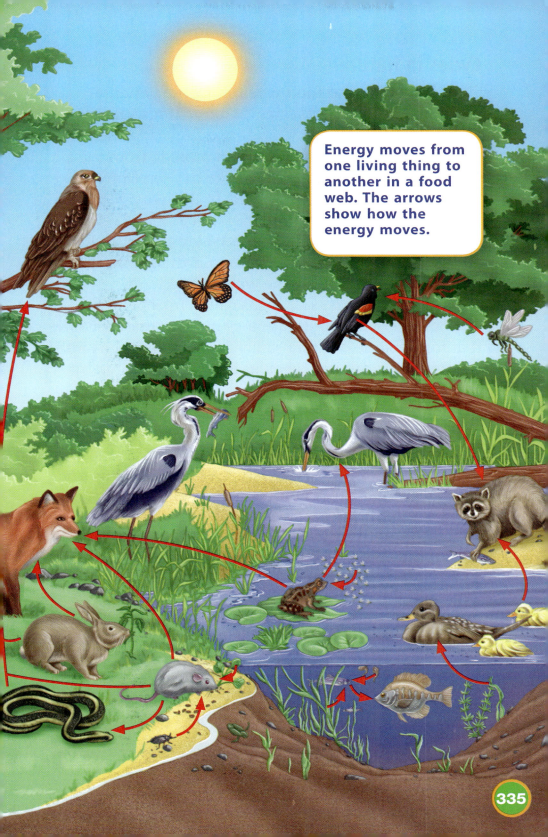

Energy moves from one living thing to another in a food web. The arrows show how the energy moves.

Cycles in Nature

Food chains and food webs show how energy moves through an ecosystem. Many things interact in ecosystems.

Plants take a gas called carbon dioxide from the air. They release oxygen. Animals take oxygen from the air. They release carbon dioxide. In this way, plants and animals help one another.

All living things need water. Water leaves Earth and goes into the air. It returns to Earth as rain, sleet, and snow. This is called the water cycle.

All living things need a gas called nitrogen. Nitrogen is in the air. But living things cannot use it in that form. Some bacteria can change nitrogen gas into a form plants can use. Then animals get nitrogen by eating plants.

Bug-eating Plants   Some soils do not have a lot of nitrogen. Some plants "eat" animals to get the nitrogen they need. When a bug touches a Venus flytrap, the plant closes its leaves. It traps the bug and uses its nitrogen.

Venus flytrap

Energy Pyramid

What happens to the food you eat? You use the energy stored in food to walk, run, and do other things. A lot of this energy leaves your body in the form of heat. Some energy is stored in your body. All living things use some energy and lose some energy. All living things store some energy.

An energy pyramid shows how energy moves through an ecosystem. Look at the energy pyramid. Each level is larger than the level above it. About 10 percent of the energy in one level moves to the next level.

Producers make up the base of the energy pyramid. First-level consumers make up the next level. Second-level and third-level consumers make up the next levels.

An energy pyramid shows how energy moves to each level of an ecosystem.

An energy pyramid helps explain the populations of ecosystems. Producers almost always have the largest populations. This is because they have the most energy to use. Next are the first-level and second-level consumers. An ecosystem can support only a few third-level consumers.

The higher an animal is on the energy pyramid, the more land it must cover to find food. Animals such as eagles, lions, and snakes have large hunting areas. These animals have special ways to move quickly and to catch smaller animals.

The energy pyramid shows why food chains are made of only three or four links. After that, there is not much energy for an animal to use.

The worm is a decomposer. The frog is a second-level consumer.

CLASSIFY

What is an energy pyramid?

Glossary

biome (BY ohm), large group of similar ecosystems

climate (KLY miht), normal pattern of weather that occurs in an area over a long period of time

community (kuh MYOO nih tee), group of living things of different species found in an ecosystem

desert (DEHZ uhrt), a very dry area

ecosystem (EHK oh sihs tuhm), all the living and nonliving things that interact with one another in a given area

food chain (food chayn), description of how energy in an ecosystem flows from one organism to another

food web (food wehb), description of all the food chains in an ecosystem

grasslands (GRAS landz), land covered by grasses with few trees

Glossary

population (pahp yuh LAY shuhn), all the members of the same type of organism living in an ecosystem

taiga (TY guh), area that has long, severe winters and short, cool summers

temperate forests (TEHM puhr iht FAWR ihstz), forests that experience four distinct seasons: summer, fall, winter, and spring

tropical rain forests (TRAHP ih kuhl RAYN FAWR ihstz), forests in regions that are very hot and very rainy

tundra (TUHN druh), Earth's coldest biome

Think About What You Have Read

Vocabulary

❶ Very limited populations survive in Earth's driest _____ .

   A) tropical rain forests

   B) grasslands

   C) taigas

   D) deserts

Comprehension

❷ What factors distinguish one biome from another?

❸ Give one example each of a producer, herbivore, carnivore, omnivore, and decomposer.

❹ Describe how energy flows through an ecosystem.

Critical Thinking

❺ Describe four ways that you interacted with living and nonliving things in ecosystems today.

Life in Ecosystems

Contents

1 What Are Habitats and Niches?

Each kind of living thing has a special niche in its habitat.

Habitats

To tell people where you live, you probably use a street address. Your address is a simple way to describe where your house is.

All living things have an "address." This is the place where they live. It is called a habitat. A **habitat** is the area where an organism lives. Everything that an organism needs to live can be found in its habitat.

Many different living things may share the same habitat. For example, zebras, lions, and many other animals live in the African savanna.

Savanna Habitat

The niche of a lion includes hunting zebras.

Niches

Workers have certain jobs to do in a factory. Organisms in a habitat have jobs to do, too. A **niche** is what an organism does in its habitat.

A niche includes where the organism lives in a habitat and how it has babies. A niche includes how an organism stays safe. Many things an organism does every day are part of its niche.

Each group of organisms in a habitat uses resources in different ways. In the savanna, zebras eat the grass. Lions do not eat grass, but they lie on the grass. Birds use the grass to build nests. Because each group uses the resources in different ways, there are enough resources for everyone. However, changes in ecosystems can upset this balance.

The niche of a zebra includes eating grass.

Adaptations

An **adaptation** is something that helps an organism survive in its environment. Some adaptations are physical. The turtles shown on this page are good examples of animals with adaptations. The desert turtle has feet that help it move easily across the sand. The sea turtle has flippers that help it move through water. Each animal's body has special parts to help it live in its habitat.

Other adaptations are things that an organism does. For example, a bat might sleep through the winter. This adaptation is called hibernation. It allows the bat to live in cold climates.

The flippers of a sea turtle are adapted for swimming.

The feet of a desert tortoise are adapted for walking in sand.

Natural Selection

In the 1800s, Charles Darwin suggested a way to help explain adaptations. Darwin said that some members of a species have features that help them live in their environment. Other members of the same species may not have these features. The members with special features are more likely to survive. Then they pass those features on to their babies.

This process is known as natural selection. Let's look at how it works.

A population of birds searches for food among the rocks on a beach. Some of the birds have long, pointed beaks. They can easily pick up food from the cracks between the rocks. Other birds have shorter, round beaks. They cannot reach the food.

The birds with the pointed beaks are more likely to stay alive. Their babies will have the same kind of beaks. After several generations, many more birds on the beach will have long, pointed beaks.

The sandpiper has a long, thin beak. This helps it get food in its habitat.

Symbiosis

All living things depend on and affect one another. Some organisms develop close relationships. <mark>Symbiosis</mark> is a close, long-lasting relationship between two different kinds of organisms.

There are three different kinds of symbiosis. The first kind is called parasitism. One organism in the relationship is helped and the other is hurt. The second kind is called commensalism. One organism is helped and the other is not affected. The third kind is called mutualism. Both organisms are helped.

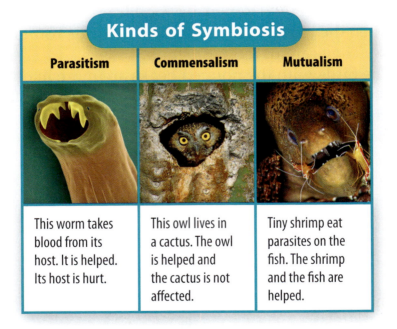

Kinds of Symbiosis

Parasitism	Commensalism	Mutualism
This worm takes blood from its host. It is helped. Its host is hurt.	This owl lives in a cactus. The owl is helped and the cactus is not affected.	Tiny shrimp eat parasites on the fish. The shrimp and the fish are helped.

COMPARE AND CONTRAST

How do habitats and niches compare?

2

What Factors Affect Ecosystems?

The size of any population can vary over time. It responds to changes in climate and resources.

A Balanced Ecosystem

Living things use resources of an ecosystem in different ways. They take some resources from ecosystems. They add others to it. A balanced ecosystem has enough resources for all of its living things.

Every ecosystem supports many populations. A **population** is all the members of the same kind of organism that live together in the same area. Any change in one part of an ecosystem can upset the balance. For example, suppose a disease kills plants that rabbits eat. This could lower the rabbit population. Animals that eat rabbits would have to find new food.

On the other hand, a large rabbit population might crowd out other species that live in the area. Because ecosystems have limited resources, they can support only a limited number of living things.

The snake eats frog eggs. This keeps the frog population from getting too large.

Limits on Population

In any ecosystem, populations are always changing. Old animals die. New ones take their place. When a tree falls, plants that need sunlight can begin to grow. However, some changes can upset the balance of an ecosystem.

Think about how predators and prey relate to one another. **Predators** are animals that hunt and eat other animals. **Prey** are animals that are hunted and eaten by predators.

In a healthy ecosystem, the number of predators and prey are balanced. But sometimes this balance is upset. One example comes from an actual ecosystem— Isle Royale, an island in Lake Superior.

Moose first appeared on the island about 1900. They may have crossed a bridge of ice from the mainland. The island had plenty of plants for the moose to eat. There were no predators.

wolf – predator

moose – prey

The population of moose grew quickly until 1930. Then it fell sharply. This was because the moose did not have enough food. Food is a limited resource in an ecosystem. So, the limited food supply on the island helped slow population growth.

In 1950, wolves appeared on the island. Wolves are predators of moose. The moose population dropped. The wolf population grew. Then the wolf population dropped because there were not enough moose left as prey. With fewer wolves, the moose population grew again.

The graph below shows the change in populations of moose and wolves on the island. The two populations tend to rise and fall together.

When there are not enough predators, an ecosystem can be unbalanced. Prey populations grow too much. Adding predators is one way to balance the ecosystem again.

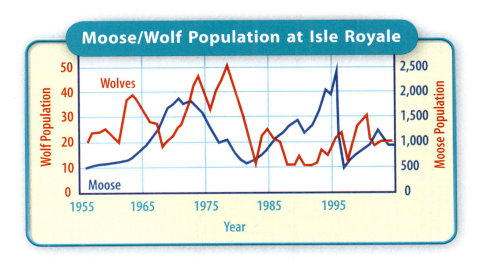

Changing the Balance

Once changed, an ecosystem may take hundreds of years to recover. In some cases, it is changed forever.

Living things can cause big changes in ecosystems. Alien species are good examples. Alien species are plants, animals, or other organisms that come into an ecosystem. They may not have any predators in this ecosystem. Sometimes they take resources from other plants and animals in the ecosystem.

For example, zebra mussels came from Russia to North America in water stored on a boat. The mussels were dumped into the Great Lakes with the water. In about ten years, the mussels have spread throughout the lakes and rivers.

Zebra mussels clog water pipes. They also grow in large groups on other animals that live in the water. Their growth can kill these animals. Zebra mussels also get rid of plankton in the water. Without plankton, there is less oxygen and food for other animals.

Zebra mussels attach themselves to freshwater clams.

Nonliving things can also change the balance of an ecosystem. These include natural events, such as volcanoes erupting.

Mount St. Helens is a volcano in the state of Washington. For many years, it was like a sleeping giant. It did not cause any trouble.

In May 1980, the volcano erupted. Hot lava burned and destroyed trees over an area of 500 square kilometers. Thick layers of ash covered the ground. Almost nothing was left in the area around the volcano.

Slowly, life returned to the mountain and nearby areas.

Other natural events include fires, floods, and times of little or no rain. Each can cause long-lasting changes in an ecosystem.

Three years after Mount St. Helens erupted, flowers began to bloom again.

1983

1980

Adapting to Change

Living things respond to big changes in their environment. Sometimes they move to a new home.

A living thing can also adapt to changes in its environment. For example, many animals grow thicker coats of fur in cold weather.

If the change is too big, the animal might die. An animal dies if it cannot adapt or move to survive a change.

Over time, living things have moved, adapted, and died. Fossils give clues to how this happened. Fossils are the remains or traces of things that once lived.

Look at the fossil shown on this page. It is not like any animals today. Dinosaurs died because they could not survive the changes in their environment.

Scientists study fossils to see how living things have changed over time.

Crest

Skull

Neck

Ribs

Leg

Arm

Evidence in Rocks

Change in an ecosystem can occur very quickly. It can affect large areas. Sometimes living things die because of change. When this happens, a species becomes extinct. **Extinction** occurs when all members of a species are gone from Earth.

Scientists can learn about extinct species by studying fossils. They also study the rocks in which the fossils were found. Fossils and rocks show that species and ecosystems have changed a great deal throughout Earth's history.

Scientists can guess the age of a fossil using a process called radioactive dating.

Sometimes the fact that there are not any fossils gives key information. For example, there are not any dinosaur fossils in rocks younger than 65 million years old. From this information, scientists think that all the dinosaurs died at about the same time. When many species die at about the same time, it is called mass extinction.

Fossils in these rock layers formed at the same time as the rocks. The oldest fossils are in the bottom layer.

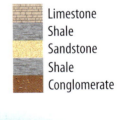

Limestone
Shale
Sandstone
Shale
Conglomerate

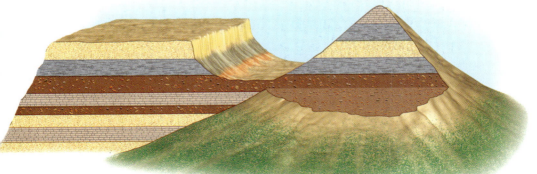

This map shows glaciers in the Northern Hemisphere during the last ice age.

Climate Change

Over the last two million years, large parts of North America and Europe have been covered many times by very large ice sheets, or glaciers. These periods are called ice ages. The last ice age ended about 11,000 years ago.

During an ice age, much of Earth's water is locked up in glaciers, causing sea levels to fall. During the last ice age, the drop in sea level exposed a land bridge between Asia and North America. Many living things, including humans, may have crossed this bridge to settle in North America.

Glacier

Equator

Many animals were already in North America at this time. Some were very large, like the saber-toothed cat. With their thick fur, they survived the cold climate. But when the ice age ended, they became extinct.

Some scientists think that these animals could not adapt to the warmer climate. Other scientists think that both climate and humans caused the extinction. Humans may have killed many of the big cats.

Scientists may never know the exact reasons why some animals become extinct. But Earth's climate does change from time to time. These changes greatly affect the living things on Earth.

CAUSE AND EFFECT

How might a decrease in predators affect prey?

3

How Can Humans Change Ecosystems?

Human activities change ecosystems in both good and bad ways.

Human Activities

Rain forests are one of the most valuable resources on Earth. They are home to many kinds of plants and animals. But rain forests are being destroyed every day.

People clear rain forests for land to grow crops and raise livestock. They also build homes and businesses there. Wood that comes from the trees is worth a lot of money.

Why should you care about the loss of the rain forests? One reason is that plants and animals may become extinct when their habitats are destroyed. Scientists think that some rain forest plants may contain things that could be used to make medicines. Rain forest plants also release oxygen and take in carbon dioxide from the air.

Tropical rain forests are being cut down. Many living things are lost along with the trees.

Builders cut the top off a hill to build these houses in California.

Humans affect ecosystems by destroying habitats. Habitat loss is the main reason why the rates of extinction are rising. Rain forests are not the only places affected. Other ecosystems are changed, too.

For example, wetlands are sometimes drained and filled. Then the land is used for farms, businesses, and houses.

Too much hunting and fishing also harms many ecosystems. In the early 1800s, more than 60 million bison, or buffalo, roamed the Great Plains. By 1890, fewer than one thousand were left. People killed the bison for their hides and other parts.

When a species is close to extinction, it is called an **endangered species**. When a species is close to becoming endangered, it is called a **threatened species**. These categories let everyone know which species need the most help.

Pollution

What other human activities can affect ecosystems? Burning fossil fuels is one example. Fossil fuels include oil, gas, and coal. These fuels contain a lot of energy and are easy to use. But burning them can cause pollution. **Pollution** is the addition of harmful things to the environment.

When fossil fuels are burned, some gases and small pieces of solids go into the air. These things are called pollutants. They can make the air unhealthy to breathe. Some combine with drops of water to form acids. They fall to the ground as acid rain.

Factories that burn fossil fuels cause some air pollution.

Sometimes fossil fuels harm the environment without being burned. Oil is often moved on big ships called tankers. Accidents may cause the oil to spill. An oil spill can damage the environment. About 300,000 birds died from a major oil spill in Alaska in 1989.

Human activities can also pollute land. Each year, people in the United States produce hundreds of millions of tons of solid waste. Solid waste includes paper, plastics, and metals. Most solid waste is buried in places called landfills. Some is burned. But people sometimes dump solid waste along roads. They throw waste into bodies of water, too.

Pollution can come from fertilizers, too. Fertilizers are chemicals. They are used on farms and lawns to make things grow. Rain can wash the fertilizers into rivers and streams. There they may damage ecosystems.

Oil spills can harm plants and animals that live in or near the water.

Growth of Human Population

Hundreds of years ago, the effects of human activities were usually small. There were no power plants or cars. The number of people was much smaller than it is today. As the graph shows, today's human population is very large. It is growing larger all the time.

Only about 1 billion people lived on Earth in 1800. By 1930 there were 2 billion people. By 1960—just 30 years later—there were 3 billion people. Today, there are more than 6 billion people.

Humans have been around for many years. Yet our population growth was fairly steady until the last 200 years. Why has the human population grown so fast in such a short time? New medicines and technology help people to survive diseases and accidents. These same things also help people live a longer time.

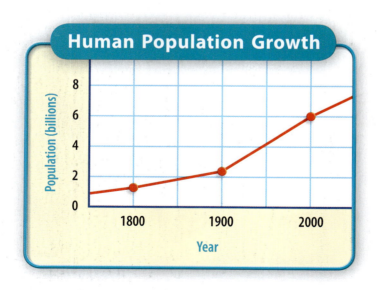

Human Population Growth

Everyone needs food, clean water, clean air, shelter, and other resources. But, as you have learned, ecosystems have limited resources. If the human population keeps growing, there will not be enough resources for everyone. In fact, today in many parts of the world, there is not enough food and water for everyone.

Remember that human activities can harm ecosystems. A growing human population will take up more space. More habitats will be lost. More species will be threatened or become extinct.

A growing human population must compete for resources such as food, land, and water.

Good News

All around the world, people are working to reduce pollution. They are trying to restore damaged ecosystems. Governments are passing laws. Businesses are taking action. And people like you are making a difference everywhere!

In the United States, wildlife refuges cover millions of acres of land. Building and hunting are limited in these areas.

People can clean up trash and plant new trees. They can use their cars less. One person can make a big difference!

DRAW CONCLUSIONS

Can the actions of one person help the environment? Explain your answer.

Glossary

adaptation (ad ap TAY shuhn), a trait or characteristic that helps an organism survive in its environment

endangered species (ehn DAYN juhrd SPEE sheez), a species close to becoming extinct

extinction (ihk STIHNGK shuhn), when all members of a species die out

habitat (HAB ih tat), the natural environment where an organism lives

niche (nihch), the role of an organism in its habitat

pollution (puh LOO shuhn), addition of harmful substances to the environment

Glossary

population (pahp you LAY shuhn), all the members of the same type of organism living in an ecosystem

predator (PREHD uh tuhr), animal that hunts and eats other animals

prey (pray), animal that is hunted and eaten by predators

symbiosis (sihm bee OH sihs), close, long-lasting relationship between species

threatened species (THREHT nd   SPEE sheez), a species close to becoming endangered

Think About What You Have Read

Vocabulary

1 An organisim's niche includes _____.

    A) where it lives

    B) how it protects itself

    C) how it reproduces

    D) all of the above

Comprehension

2 Describe two different niches in a savanna habitat.

3 What can scientists learn by studying fossils and rocks?

4 How has the growth in human population affected ecosystems around the world?

Critical Thinking

5 What are some things you can do to help the environment? How could you encourage people to join you?

Index

Electric current, 90, 92–93, 146, 165

Electric generator, 148–149, 165

Electricity

from batteries and fuel cells, 146–147

change of energy form and, 101, 160

conductors of, 13, 14, 15, 37

distribution of, 164

electric motors, 162–163

in home heating systems, 138

as kinetic energy, 102

noble gases and, 16

production of, 144, 148–151

static electricity, 144–145, 166

thermal energy and, 128

uses for, 160–164

Electric motors, 162–163, 165

Electromagnetic energy, 100–101

Electromagnetic spectrum, 114–115

Electromagnetic waves, 114–115, 134–135

Electromagnets, 92–93, 95, 162–163

Electrons, 5, 6, 24

auroras and, 94

electric circuits and, 152

electricity and, 144–145

magnetism and, 90–91

El Niño, 201, 209

Endangered species, 359, 365

Endocrine system, 284, 285

Endoplasmic reticulum, 260, 261, 263

Energy, 100, 121

alternate energy sources, 172–173

change in form, 100

changes of states and, 34, 35, 64–68

chemical, 100, 101, 102

chemical reactions and, 19

conservation of, 100

control of in the body, 284

of elasticity, 102

electrical, 101, 102

electromagnetic, 100, 135

from fossil fuels, 170–171

hydroelectric, 149, 172

kinetic and potential, 100, 102–103

mechanical, 101, 102

mitochondrion and, 262

movement through the food chain and food web, 333–338

as need of living things, 266

photosynthesis and, 274, 292, 294, 297, 332

Credits

Photography and Illustration Credits

2 © The Granger Collection, New York. **3** © PhotoDisc, Inc. **4** © The Granger Collection, New York. **5–6** Bill Melvin. **(illustrations)** Bill Melvin. **(tl)** © Lawrence Lawry/SPL/Photo Researchers, Inc. **(tr)** © HMCo/Allan Landau. **8 (t)** © PhotoDisc, Inc. **(b)** © Eyewire/Photodisc, Inc./Punch Stock. **9 (l)** © Photolibrary Ltd./Index Stock Imagery. **(r)** © Comstock Images/Alamy Images. **11** © The Granger Collection, New York. **14 (l)** © G. Brad Lewis/SPL/Photo Researchers, Inc. **(r)** © Earth Scenes. **15 (r)** © Joel Greenstein/Omni-Photo Communications. **(l)** © R-R/Grant Heilman Photography, Inc. **16 (r)** © Andrew Lambert Photography/SPL/Photo Researchers, Inc. **(l)** © Burr Lewis/Democrat and Chronicle/AP Wide World Photo. **17** © Jack Anderson/Picture Arts/Corbis. **(illustration)** Bill Melvin. **18** © Ton Koene/Visuals Unlimited, Inc. **19–20** © HMCo/Charles Winters. **21** © Richard Megna/Fundamental Photographs. **22 (b)** © Dave King/Dorling Kindersley Picture Library. **(c)** © Peter Harholdt/Corbis. **(t)** © David Wrobel/Visuals Unlimited, Inc. **(illustrations)** Bill Melvin. **23–25** Bill Melvin. **28** © HMCo/Charles Winters. **29** © HMCo/Allan Landau. **30** © HMCo/Allan Landau. **32–34** © HMCo/Charles Winters. **(illustration)** George V. Kelvin. **35** © HMCo/Charles Winters. **(illustration)** George V. Kelvin. **36** © HMCo/Charles Winters. **37** © Sheila Terry/SPL/Photo Researchers, Inc. **38** © HMCo/Allan Landau. **39** © MedioImagesPunch Stock. **40** © HMCo/Charles Winters. **41** © HMCo/Allan Landau. **42–43** © Wally Eberhart/Visuals Unlimited, Inc. **44** © Food Collection/Punch Stock. **45** © HMCo/Allan Landau. **46–47** © Lawrence Stepanowicz/Panographics. **47 (inset)** Bill Melvin. **48** © Somboon-UNEP/Peter Arnold, Inc. **49(t)** © Angelo Cavalli/Index Stock Imagery. **(br)** © Mauro Fermariello/SPL/Photo Researchers, Inc. **(bl)** © Philip Gould/Corbis. **(m)** © Jeremy Bishop/SPL/Photo Researchers, Inc. **50** © Tony Freeman/PhotoEdit, Inc. **51** © Wally Eberhart/Visuals Unlimited, Inc. **52 (t)** © HMCo/Allan Landau. **(b)** © Lawrence Stepanowicz/Panographics. **54** © Allsport Concepts/Getty Images. **55** © Michael Alberstat/Masterfile. **56–57** © Russell Monk/Masterfile. **(illustrations)** George V. Kelvin. **58** © Allsport Concepts/Getty Images. **59** © HMCo/Allan Landau. **60–62** © Fundamental Photographs. **64** © Roy Toft/National Geographic Image Collection. **65** © Michael Alberstat/Masterfile. **66 (tr)** © Bill Boch/Botanica/Getty Images. **(bl)** © Fundamental Photographs. **67** © Tom Uhlman/Visuals Unlimited, Inc. **68** George V. Kelvin. **69 (t)** © Michael Alberstat/Masterfile. **(b)** © Bill Boch/Botanica/Getty Images. **70 (t)** © Fundamental Photographs. **(b)** © Tom Uhlman/Visuals Unlimited, Inc. **72** © Brand-X Pictures/ Punch Stock. **73** © ImageState-Pictor/PictureQuest. **74** Bill Melvin. **75** © Brand-X Pictures/Punch Stock. **76 (l)** © Osf/M. Hill/Animals Animals. **(lm)** © Phillip Colla/SeaPics. **(rm)** © Mark Payne-Gill/Nature Picture Library. **(r)** © Nancy Rotenberg/Animals Animals. **77** © Heinz Kluetmeier/Sports Illustrated/Figure Skater Brian Boitano, 1988. **78–79** © HMCo/Lawrence Migdale. **80** © ImageState-Pictor/PictureQuest. **81 (r)** ©Michael Newman/PhotoEdit, Inc. **(l)** © Michael Newmam/PhotoEdit, Inc. **82** © HMCo/Lawrence Migdale. **83** Bill Melvin. **84 (t)** Bill Melvin. **(b)** © Dorling Kindersley Picture Library. **85–86** Bill Melvin. **87 (inset)** © Jeffrey Greenberg/Photo Researchers, Inc. **88 (t)** © Ned Therrien/Visuals Unlimited, Inc. **(b)** © HMCo/Lawrence Migdale. **89 (l)** © Artville. **(r)** © Phil Crabbe/Dorling Kindersley Picture Library. **90** © HMCo/Lawrence Migdale. **(illustrations)** Ron Carboni. **91** © Spencer Grant/PhotoEdit, Inc. **92** ©HMCo/Allan Landau. **93 (tl)** © Van Dykes Restorers. **(bell)** Bill Melvin. **94** © Chris Madeley/SPL/Photo Researchers, Inc. **95 (t)** © Brand-X Pictures/Punch Stock. **(b)** © Michael Newman/PhotoEdit, Inc. **96 (t)** © Heinz Kluetmeier/Sports Illustrated/Figure Skater Brian Boitano, 1988. **(b)** © Osf/M. Hill/Animals Animals. **98–99** © HMCo/Allan Landau. **100** © Bob Daemmerich/Corbis. **101** © Corbis. **103** © HMCo/Allan Landau. **104** © Loren M. Winters. **105** © Fukuhara, Inc/Corbis. **106–107** © HMCo/Allan Landau. **109** © Phil McCarter/PhotoEdit, Inc. **112** © Gibson Stock Photography **113** © View Pictures Ltd./Alamy Images. **115 (b)** © ACE Photo Agency/Robertstock. **(t)** Mike Saunders. **116** © Churchill and Klehr. **117** © SIU/Visuals Unlimited, Inc. **118–119** Mike Saunders. **120** © Stockbyte/SuperStock. **121 (t)** © Corbis. **(b)** © HMCo/Allan Landau. **122 (t)** © Churchill and Klehr. **(m)** © SIU/Visuals Unlimited, Inc. **(b)** © ACE Photo Agency/Robertstock. **124–126** © HMCo/Allan Landau. **(insets)** George V. Kelvin. **127 (illustration)** George V. Kelvin. **(t)** © David Young Wolff/PhotoEdit, Inc. **(tm)** © Comstock Images/Getty. **(bm)** © Japack Company/Corbis. **(b)** © HMCo/Allan Landau. **128** © HMCo/Charles Winters. **129-130** © HMCo/Allan Landau. **131** © Creatas. **132** © HMCo/Charles Winters. **133** © HMCo/Allan Landau. **134** © Kindra Clineff/PictureQuest. **135** George V. Kelvin. **136** © HMCo/Charles Winters. **137 (l)** © Ted Kinsman/Photo Researchers, Inc. **(r)** © Tony Freeman/PhotoEdit, Inc. **138** George V. Kelvin. **139 (t)** © HMCo/Charles Winters. **(m)** © HMCo/Allan Landau. **(b)** © HMCo/Allan Landau. **140 (t)** © Kindra Clineff/PictureQuest. **(b)** George V. Kelvin. **142** © Dmitriy Margolin/D Photography. **(illustration)** Slim Films. **143** © Bob Daemmrich/The Image Works. **144–145** © HMCo/Allan Landau. **146–147** © Dmitriy Margolin/D Photography. **(illustration)** Slim Films. **148 (d)** © Science Photos/Alamy Images Ltd. **(br)** Slim Films. **149** © Mike Mullen. **150** Slim Films. **151** © Michael Melford/The Image Bank/Getty Images. **152** © Barrie Rokeach. **153** © HMCo/Allan Landau. **154** © Corbis. **155–157** © HMCo/Charles Winters. **158** © Dennis Boothroyd/EcoStock. **159 (t)** © Will Powers. **160 (t)** © Ken Chernus/Taxi/Getty Images. **161 (t)** © Chris Cheadle/The Image Bank/Getty Images. **(b)** © HMCo/Allan Landau. **162** Slim Films. **163** © Bob Daemmrich/The Image Works. **164** Slim Films. **165 (t)** © HMCo/Charles Winters. **(m)** Slim Films. **(b)** Slim Films. **166 (t)** © HMCo/Charles Winters. **(m)** © HMCo/Charles Winters. **(b)** © HMCo/Charles Winters. **168-169** © HMCo/Allan Landau. **170–171** Joel Dubin. **172 (l)** © Julien Frebet/Peter Arnold, Inc. **(r)** © AFP Photo/Jeff Haynes/Getty Images. **173 (t)** © Russ Curtis/Photo Researchers, Inc. **(b)** © Corbis/Punch Stock. **174** © Eyewire/ PhotoDisc, Inc/Punch Stock. **176 (1, m)** © Sheila Terry/Science Photo Library. **(r)** Corbis. **177 (inset)** ©Jim Brandenburg/Minden Pictures. **(b)** Pat Rossi. **178** Pat Rossi. **179** © Doug Wechsler/Earth Scenes. **180** © Larry Lefever/Giant Heilman Photography, Inc. **182** © Three Lions/Getty Images. **184** © HMCo/Allan Landau. **(inset)** © HMCo/Allan Landau. **186** © Anne Dowie/Anne Dowie Index Stock Imagery. **187** © HMCo/Allan Landau. **188–189** Joe LeMonnier. **190** © Billy Barnes/Transparencies, Inc. **191** Joel Dubin. **192** Pat Rossi. **194** © Chris Cheadle/The Image Bank/Getty Images. **195** © Denny Eilers/Grant Heilman Photography. **196** Slim Films. **197 (b)** © John Foster/Masterfile Stock Photo Library. **(c)** © Bob Krist/Corbis. **(t)** © Chris Cheadle/The Image Bank/Getty Images.